NEVER LET THEM KISS YOU

A Dark Fairy Tale

C. A. Powell

CONTENTS

CHAPTER 1

WHAT A GLORIOUS MORNING

Old Arthur Ballantyne got up on the most beautiful of summer days. A fine mid-August morning during his eighty-first year of life. The garden flowers were in fine bloom and he enjoyed the cascade of colour as he looked out of the kitchen window while pouring water into his electric kettle. The cloudless sky was a glorious blue. The sort of blue that made an individual glad to be alive.

'Time for a brew,' he muttered to himself as he plugged the kettle in and the element started to heat the water. He fumbled in his bread bin and took two slices for his electric toaster, then he reached up to the cupboard for his raspberry jam. He lingered for another moment to look out over his garden and the woodland beyond.

'Today will be my last day,' he whispered to himself. 'I wonder what is beyond?'

There was a sad tear of joy in his eyes as he put the toaster on and placed an empty plate in readiness. He took out his handkerchief and dabbed the tears while whispering to himself, 'How can a person be happy and cry at the same time?'

He thought of the many delightful things that had happened in his life, then turned to look at a small, framed photo on the wall. His late wife. A lady who had given him a son and a daughter. His eyes watered again and he whispered to the photo on the wall.

'Not long now, love.'

Once again, he looked out of the window and smiled for the magnificent summer morning. He would take his tea and toast outside on the little garden table and enjoy the sun. He'd be able to look out on his garden for the last time. His cherished New Forest cottage was always resplendent at this time of year – his wonderful abode was gorgeous and he'd lived a splendid life. Today would be his glorious twilight of days, and Arthur Ballantyne knew it. Why he knew was beyond reason to him. He just had a sixth sense of it all. There had been odd little dizzy turns over the past few weeks and he was beginning to feel his age. Today, he felt fine but he knew it would be for the last time. It was the plain and simple truth. It was his time and this wonderful summer day was with him for the final stretch.

The toaster pinged as the kettle boiled. Arthur went about his preparation of morning tea and toast. In a short time, he was walking out of the back door into his garden holding a tray with his little morning repast upon it.

The birds were singing and he looked over to his bird feeders and smiled. Little sparrows and blue tits were flapping about greedily at the seed he left for them. He surveyed beyond and up into the clear blue sky – no sign of the regular sparrow hawk that occasionally swooped in for the kill. The bird tables seemed to draw the predator like a magnet. Most of the time the raptor's efforts were in vain and it would move on, but now and then a naive fledgling would fall victim. A low-level swoop and then the panic among the elders before life and death moved on.

Arthur sighed acceptingly and whispered to himself, 'Sadly, it is the natural order of things.'

He placed his tray on the table and sat down. He picked up his teacup and blew before taking a tentative sip. It was still hot, which was fine. He could nibble on his toast while letting it cool. He buttered his toast and then applied some raspberry jam. Having just completed the task, he sat up with a look of delight.

'Awe! Hello, old Amy. Top of the morning to you,' he said with a broad smile.

The old female barn owl glided towards the woodland beyond the garden. She turned her head to nonchalantly look at the familiar human as she flew by.

Arthur called after the old lady owl. 'Unusual for you, my dear. There's been a lot of daylight already. I would have thought you'd be home and asleep for the day by now. When you wake tonight, I'll no longer be here. It'll not matter to you. Life goes on.' He chuckled and bit the toast with its generous and delicious spread of raspberry jam.

He sat back and crunched his toast some more, relishing the sweet, fruity tang. Then tried another sip of tea. Oh, the joys of forest life in summer. How very lucky he had been and how pleased he was to know there was no fear. A slight trepidation, but no sense of panic. He was going to die today and it would be a gentle passing away. He would sit down somewhere and fall asleep. Not in his garden. He had already made up his mind that it wouldn't be in his house or his garden.

Arthur decided he would take a walk through the side wood next to the cottage where he would emerge onto the heathland rise. At the top of the heath would be the copse of trees. The place he called the Little Wood.

He took a deep breath after putting his teacup down. 'Ah! The special place where the strange little things live.'

For a moment, Arthur took time to ponder the strange little beings that were livelier in winter snow. He thought of the strange couple, Abigail and Raymond, who never believed a word he said about them. The Wiccan couple who indulged him with strange spells and potions from an old book that worked. Spells that Abigail and Raymond didn't believe in, but they worked anyway.

Arthur turned thoughts of the Little Wood's strange little dwellers over in his mind and muttered to himself, 'One can often hear the strange little beings. One might see signs of recent presence, but to actually see them in summer is beyond rare. I never have. One never sees them during the vibrant seasons. Even autumn is barren of their sweet little giggles and laughter. Only in winter and especially during the snow, could anyone see them in their pure form. I wonder if the delightful little things will see me once more before I leave?'

He took another bite of his toast and sat back to contemplate the matter. Perhaps the little things might make an exception for him? It was his last day.

The morning sun shone down upon the garden filling Arthur with kind thoughts of all the summers he had spent in the cottage. He had lived there for over forty years. Thirty of them with his wife. For a short time, at the beginning, his son and daughter were there too. After a few years, they had moved away to start their own lives. His daughter in New Zealand, while his son lived in Salisbury – not too far away and he often visited.

The time passed pleasantly for an hour. Then Arthur gathered up the tray and went back to the house. He washed and dried his plate, teacup and saucer. He put them away and returned the raspberry jam to the cupboard. Everything was meticulously done.

The house was neat and tidy as he went to the coat rack and took out his walking stick. He also took his well-worn blue floppy bucket hat, and went to the front door. As Arthur opened it, he took one more look at his lovely cottage and smiled. His eyes were watering and he felt the pang of sadness – the finality of moving on.

He stepped out into the sunny day and slammed the door. The birds were singing their summer song as he ambled along the footpath, wiping his eyes with his trusted handkerchief. Before he had finished drying his nostalgic tears, he was strolling through the side wood.

'They used to come as far as here,' he whispered to his late wife. 'Up until Abigail's spells stopped the little things becoming too adventurous. Now they stay at the Little Wood all of the time. Their little island in the heathland.'

He stopped for a moment and looked up into the green overhanging leaves. He breathed in the warm morning air and felt very invigorated. Despite such well-being, he still knew this was his last day.

'I wonder if they would grant me an audience? Perhaps they might know too? They do appear in snow. That's when they come out most of all. Brazen little things in snow.' He chuckled.

Smiling to himself, Arthur shook his head and ambled on through the side wood. Soon he emerged upon the open heathland – another place of rustic allure. How he would miss the heaths too. He hadn't thought of this until standing before the ferns. He allowed a moment of contemplation before making his way up the path towards the copse of trees on the summit of the small hill. He usually toiled and often had to stop for a breather. But today he seemed able to keep walking, as though his strange calling had given him a hidden strength.

In a short space of time, Arthur stood before the perimeter of the Little Wood. It was only a brief moment of lingering before he entered the mystical place. The foliage and the soil all seemed to have a magical vibrance – an allure that swam within him. He smiled and ambled deeper into the wood for a few seconds.

Then, as he stopped, his face lit up with delight. Pure exaltation as he heard little giggles all around him in the shrubs and in the trees. A high-pitched snigger above as something unseen disturbed the branches and leaves before shooting off. A blur of rapid movement deep into the thick, leafy foliage. Another immature titter, then the shrubs beside him shook from something that had rapidly abandoned the position.

'Oh, my word,' said Arthur. 'I think you know. I suspected you little things might know too. Was it the forever-smitten fairy kiss that Abigail cured me of? Does something still remain?'

He looked up into the trees again. Desperately, he hoped for a final glimpse of the beautiful and wicked little creatures of the Little Wood.

'Here is my spot, you little rascals,' he chuckled humorously, 'I'm going to sit down here and hope for the best.'

And so, Arthur Ballantyne slowly lowered himself to the forest floor and sat there with a contented smile on his face. He beamed with delight when he suddenly heard the distant chanting of infantile creatures. Far off but getting closer.

'*La, la, la. La, la, la.*'

'Oh, you're such wonderful little things,' he called excitedly. 'Come and show yourselves to me? One last time? Look, look into my eyes, they make stars look dull in night-time skies. Go on, repeat that, like the little parrots you are.'

'*La, la, la. La, la, la.*'

'That's right,' he encouraged. 'Come on now. I would be delighted to look upon you one last time.'

'*La, la, la. La, la, la.*'

The chanting grew gently louder and was coming from all directions within the wood. It was closing in on Arthur's position. Suddenly plants began to grow up out of the forest floor at speed. From seed to maturing green stems like a speeded-up nature film documentary. Within mere seconds flowers were in vibrant full bloom under the forest's leafy canopy.

'Everything is invigorated in your lovely presence,' he called with tears of joy running down his cheeks. 'Go on, let me hear you say it. Look, look into my eyes. They make stars look dull in night-time skies.'

A rustle of leaves made him look towards some parting shrubs. The rhythmic chanting was still closing in and growing gently louder.

'*La, la, la. La, la, la.*'

Arthur's face lit up with sheer enchantment. 'Oh, you resplendent little pets. This is unusual of you all.'

He looked up through the leaves and made out some of the blue sky beyond. What a lovely and glorious life he had lived. What a dazzling send-off too.

CHAPTER 2

A TOKEN OF RESPECT

'Why now?' asked Abigail Chalkley as she drove the old Toyota Townace along the forest roads in the heavy snowfall. 'Why wait until it's snowing? Why wait five months to do this? You don't even believe in this Wiccan stuff.'

'Oh, so you're referring to your beliefs as "stuff" now,' answered Raymond Cheeseman, and then he added, 'Admittedly, for me, it's a bit of a whim for the old boy. He always said the strange folk of the Little Wood were more active in the snow. It's a kindly indulgence – a bypassing of actuality for a misguided old friend. Let's be honest here, Mr Ballantyne did struggle against realism. You've made the straw ornament with the symbol and written another new spell out. You've contributed too. That's three indulgent Wiccan spells you've done for him now.'

Abigail slowly turned the van along the bend in the road, careful of the snowy sludge and the chance of skidding off the lane. 'I'm all for the spell, but we could have done this back in August when Mr Ballantyne passed away.'

'I know Abigail, but seeing as Mr Ballantyne had a thing about these creatures in the snow, I thought it would be a nice gesture for him. After all, we both had a fondness for the eccentric old sod.'

'You do have a rather rude way of expressing things, Raymond.'

'And you do have some airs and graces, Abigail.' Raymond smiled. His long, straggly, greasy grey hair hung down past his hooked nose on his skinny, wrinkled fifty-nine-year-old face and on beyond his coat collar.

'You don't even believe in anything Wiccan. You indulge me and go along with my things, but you never really believe them,' scolded Abigail mildly as she straightened the vehicle along a less sleety patch of road. Her hair fell just past her shoulders. It was dark brown with bits of grey and a dyed streak of purple. She liked tint and her long cardigan of rainbow colours gave her that New Age latter-day hippy look. There she sat, with her thick, heavy-duty high-waisted and multi-dyed harem trousers. She always wore bright colours and had a selection of decorative low-crotch leg wear. Raymond always joked that her attire did wonders for his migraines.

'If the truth be said, Abby, neither do you. You certainly never believed Mr Ballantyne and his fairy stories. Your logic kicks in good and proper when things are too far off the radar of reality. Even for you and your Wiccan eccentricities.'

Abigail nodded and replied, 'Well of course. But that's what makes me puzzled by you choosing today to do this Wiccan spell for Mr Ballantyne in the snow. Usually, you would have been happy to lay the stone in nice weather and then bugger off. A mere indulgence on your part. You're going the extra mile with this little spell on the plaited Wiccan plate.'

'I think the only reason Mr Ballantyne came to us, is because of that lady quack councillor type.'

'You mean Sandy Lock. Harry Lock's young wife. They live in Lymington.'

'That's the one. The pretty mixed-race lady with the mad cascading pixie curls. Looks like that Halle Berry, the American film star. She told our Mr Ballantyne about us. She thinks we're a couple of oddball, slightly off-the-radar people. She advised him about you and your Wiccan stuff. That's why he came to us when we were in the high street by the shops that day. He even had the audacity to call us Chalk and Cheese. There's diplomacy for you.'

Abigail snorted and then grinned. 'I don't think Sandy Lock would advise Mr Ballantyne to see us in that type of way. She probably mentioned it during a professional consultation with the old man, especially if he was rambling on about mythical folklore stuff. As for his "chalk and cheese" approach, most of the people of Lymington refer to us as Chalk and Cheese for two reasons. Obviously, our surnames of Chalkley and Cheeseman, and because you speak like an uneducated oaf and—'

'You get to be the educated duchess with your airs and graces in your New Age baggy attire and multi-streaked hair colouring that changes from one month to the next,' Raymond interceded to get his point of view in first.

'Well, it all adds up to a chalk and cheese couple.' She chuckled.

'I suppose it does,' agreed Raymond with a contented smile. 'I wouldn't have it any other way. And I keep telling myself that one day, one of your magic Wiccan spells will win me over. Here we are at the wrong end of our fifties, still living an outdated latter-day hippy dream.'

Abigail laughed. 'A spell that you might believe works. I'll look forward to the day when that happens. Never say never, Raymond.'

Abigail pulled the van over into an inlet of icy gravel. The other side of the slushy gritted road was all forest, but there was an area of heath, where the van had stopped. The heathland ascended to a small copse of trees, an island surrounded by a sea of gorgeous fluffy snow. To this frosty carpet was the additional snowfall. It was hard to see through the winter surge, but Raymond and Abigail knew the small wood was at the heath's summit – their ultimate destination for the task at hand.

'This is the place, though it looks different in the snow,' said Raymond.

'The side wood is over there and the late Mr Ballantyne's cottage is beyond,' answered Abigail. 'I wonder if anyone has bought the place?'

'Your second special Wiccan spell will no longer protect the cottage now there are new owners,' added Raymond sarcastically. 'I remember you saying that.'

'Well, it doesn't matter now. Mr Ballantyne believed such things and he's gone. If new people have purchased the cottage, I'm sure they're not as off the radar as the dear old late Mr Ballantyne was.'

'Or as off the radar as us?' added Raymond with a raised eyebrow.

Abigail playfully clouted him and got out of the van. She walked around to the sliding door as Raymond got out. The cold hail was still falling all about them and the rising heathland was breathtaking with its white blanket of thick snow. The ferns were gradually disappearing beneath the cascading flurry. Abigail bent inside and pulled out a circular woven straw-spiral plate. There was a triangular diagram painted on it and each corner had a twisting outer pattern. A small note lay upon it – the written spell.

'You've translated it into Irish Gaelic again. Why do you always do that?' asked Raymond, laughing. 'No one can understand it.'

'I was once told it's more authentic and the old Witchcraft book, I bought, also explains that the ancient language carries certain merit. Often incantations are best recited and written in the old language,' added Abigail.

'But you can't speak Irish Gaelic,' said Raymond.

'No, but there's a translator on Google and the Witchcraft book shows the spells and pronunciations in Gaelic too. I can understand what each one means via the translator, but prefer to leave all incantations in Gaelic,' Abigail answered.

'Even though you don't believe them?' added Raymond, tormenting.

'It is all part of the protocol,' added Abigail tartly.

'But this Wiccan incantation is one I looked up and it was in English anyway. It's not from your book, but you still translated it into Gaelic.' Raymond was amused and teasing Abigail.

'I always make sure the incantation is in Gaelic. You know that.' Abigail pinned the note upon the circular, woven straw plate, above the painted triangular symbol.

'Can I look at it?' asked Raymond.

'If you must,' she replied as the white flakes fell all about them.

Raymond looked at the pinned paper and tried to see if any of the words were recognisable to English.

Scaoilim mé féin uathu siúd a d'fhág an eitleán seo,
Agus lig dóibh siúl gairdíní beannaithe Summerland.

Abigail raised her eyes to the falling snow when Raymond's face lit up. Something further to mock, no doubt.

'Why is Summerland written as "Summerland" in Irish Gaelic? Surely Gaelic has a word for "summer" and "land"?'

'They do, unless it's an actual place with a name. The name remains constant,' hissed Abigail as she snatched the woven Wiccan plate from him. She slid the people carrier's door shut with an irritated slam and proceeded along the snowy path up towards the Little Wood.

She turned and called back, 'In written Gaelic, Little Wood would still be called Little Wood in spelling and pronunciation. Because Little Wood is its name. Gaelic has a name for the words "little" and "wood" but the place name remains constant in all languages. Even if it was said in Outer Mongolian.'

Raymond followed her through the falling snow and called irritatingly, 'Getting a tad touchy, aren't we? It was just a question. A little thing I happened to notice.'

'At times, Raymond, I think you would notice a pimple on an elephant's arse at a thousand yards.'

'Oh, pardon me.' He laughed as he followed her up the snowy slope. All the white-covered ferns looked alluring with the onslaught of falling snow-flakes. Gradually, they worked their way up the slope with the Little Wood looming larger before them.

'A lot different from the summer,' he called, looking at the bare branches through the white slurry.

'Much different,' agreed Abigail, her happy mood back.

Such moments of irritation lasted for a short period of time. It's what Raymond loved about his eccentric old girlfriend. She didn't believe in Christian marriage but they had done the Wiccan ceremony, an outdoor affair with guests inside a circle and candles. There had been invocations of various Earth elements for the occasion. Raymond had gone along with it all for Abigail. It didn't mean anything to him and perhaps Abigail knew it was an indulgence on his part. But he loved her dearly anyway. His eccentric woman who put up with him and his shortcomings. Raymond had to admit, he was rather good on the shortcomings front.

He looked back down through the snow and saw a man walking along the lane with a black dog.

'Hey, someone does live in Mr Ballantyne's old home. I think that man with the dog must have come out of there.'

Abigail stopped to look down through the snow-fall. She saw the man slow down as he passed their parked people carrier. He looked up intuitively towards their position, then continued past the parked vehicle and on with his dog walk.

'Looks like a bit of a snooty git, if you ask me,' said Raymond.

'Everyone starts off on a snooty git list with you. In fact, a person must work hard to get off of it,' said Abigail, chuckling.

'Well, I bet he'd have his work cut out to get off of it,' replied Raymond humorously.

He turned and continued to ascend through the falling snow towards the copse of trees. Abigail quickened her pace and caught up. She trudged on, beside Raymond, knowing there'd be something else for him to talk about. She always knew when he was in one of his continuously inquisitive moods. Sure enough, he asked her another question.

'What always puzzled me, is why and how Mr Ballantyne got another bee in his bonnet about

the second spell inside his house. You know, to counter the "sweet spot attraction", as he put it.'

Abigail was sure she'd answered such a question before, but she indulged him all the same.
'He didn't invent such words. They were in the
book, in the chapter on wraiths and sprites. Mr
Ballantyne was reading the whole chapter when
I was mixing the potion to stop the effects of the
forever-smitten kiss. Later, he decided to have the
second spell to be on the safe side. We were of
course indulging him from a psychological point
of view. Therefore, I complied with his wish and
let him watch me do the second spell, to put his
troubled mind at rest. This supposedly stopped
the little urchins of the Little Wood visiting his
cottage or breaking in.'

Raymond sniggered. 'The bloody strange thing
is, it seemed to work for the old fella.'

'It worked in the sense that Mr Ballantyne was
no longer neurotic with fear about his imagined little folk. But he continued to insist such mischievous
sprites were living in this Little Wood.'

'Well and truly away with the fairies was the late
Mr Ballantyne,' added Raymond derisively.

'Sometimes I curse the day I came across that
old book,' Abigail said with a groan.

'You don't mean that,' added Raymond with a
smile. 'You often say it's fine apart from that one
wraiths and sprites chapter. It seems to take all the

kind spells of love and ailments seriously and then takes a break to go completely bizarre for wraiths and sprites before going back to being normal with straightforward potions for real types of complaint.'

'Yes,' she agreed as they trudged upwards through the snow. 'There are those more worthy things within the book, I suppose.'

They got to the perimeter of the Little Wood and went into the trees. Snow still fell through the overhanging branches, though the fall was not as intense. They moved into a small clearing, smelling the freshness of the frosty place.

'We can put it up here,' said Abigail. She pulled down a branch and tried to twist a wet twig from the thin stem in order to slide the wicker handle of the woven straw plate onto the branch, where it might hang.

'Let me do that, Abigail.' Raymond moved forward and got out his lock knife. He cut the wet twig with the sharp blade and then stabbed the knife into the tree's bark while hanging the symbolic circular straw plate, complete with the written Gaelic incantation. He looked back at her and smiled.

'How's that?' he asked.

Abigail was frowning and looking past him. Something had caught her interest.

'That's strange,' said Abigail as she walked over to a small patch of flowers growing through the snow. 'How can these grow and bloom in winter?'

Raymond frowned and walked over to stand beside her. 'They can't grow now, surely. Not in mid-winter. They're cornflowers. I don't think they grow in forests anyway. Are they real?' He bent down to touch one and recoiled as the petals began to wilt and rapidly age before his very eyes. He stood up and stepped back.

'That is bloody spooky,' he muttered.

'I've never seen anything like that happen before,' added Abigail.

Together, they stood there transfixed. What a strange sight – the blue cornflowers suddenly withering and putrefying before their very eyes. It was a strange and displeasing spectacle.

'That is so sad. What on earth caused that?' whispered Abigail in startled awe.

'I don't know,' Raymond replied. 'It's the strangest thing I've ever seen. And there was something horribly desolate about it.'

Far off, and deeper into the wood, came the chanting of distant infantile voices.

'*La, la, la. La, la, la.*'

'Can you hear that?' hissed Abigail.

''It's the bluster of the snow outside of the wood,' replied Raymond. He was clearly agitated. 'Let's get back to the van, Abigail. We'll be jumping at our own shadows soon.'

'*La, la, la. La, la, la.*'

'Yes, I'd like to be away from here now. This feels a little spooky,' agreed Abigail.

They wasted no time getting out of the Little Wood and descending the snowy heathland amid the falling snow. There was a slight wind now and the white flakes were swirling a little more vigorously. The descent was much quicker than the ascent. By the time they reached their parked people carrier the whole strange incident was little more than a silly distant memory, an unearthly noise of the wind.

'Hello there,' called a voice to their side. It was the dog walker returning with his black Labrador. The mutt was pulling excitedly at the lead wanting to make friends with the strange people.

'Calm down, Nelly,' scolded the man softly. 'She's a bit excitable.'

'Hello,' replied Abigail.

'Alright there, mate?' said Raymond.

'You sound like you come from my neck of the woods,' replied the dog walker with his London accent.

'I'm from Hammersmith, originally,' said Raymond.

'I'm from Bow,' replied the man with a laugh.

'Have you moved into the cottage next to these side woods?' asked Abigail.

'Yes, on the thirtieth of December, would you believe. We've been in a couple of weeks now,' replied the dog walker.

'We knew Mr Ballantyne, who lived there before,' added Abigail. 'We just put a small memorial to him up in the Little Wood. He passed away up there in August with a very peaceful smile upon his face, we were told.'

'Oh,' said the dog walker. 'You certainly picked a strange day for it.'

'It was for Mr Ballantyne,' said Abigail, laughing jovially. 'He always said the little folk came out in the snow. He was of the same type of Wiccan belief as us. An interest that we shared.'

Raymond closed his eyes and sighed. Abigail sometimes trusted people a little too much with her beliefs. There she was in all her eccentric hippy gear and her multi-coloured hair mentioning little folk to someone she has met a few seconds ago.

'Oh, right,' replied the dog walker. His friendly enthusiasm suddenly lessened. 'Well, it's nice to meet you. I better be getting the old girl indoors. All the best.'

They watched as the man walked on towards the Little Wood beyond which was the old cottage, where the late Mr Ballantyne once lived and now the dog walker resided.

Abigail climbed into the driver's seat as Raymond got into the passenger side.

'Well, he seemed to be warm and then aloof,' said Abigail.

'You laid the late Mr Ballantyne's "strange forest folk" thing on him twenty seconds into meeting the fella, then the Wiccan stuff. You're supposed to feel someone out first. It takes time. It's not something you casually put on someone when first meeting them, Abigail. It goes down like a fart at a royal banquet.'

'Oh, why must you be so crude and vulgar about things, Raymond. Fancy putting it like that,' scolded Abigail as she wrinkled up her nose and started the vehicle.

CHAPTER 3

THE LATE MR BALLANTYNE

Janice Careful flicked back her short thin fair hair as she sat down at the kitchen table. She had a slight boyish look with her neatly cut fringe that separated the two sides of a short, layered bob-style cut. Her friend, Sandy Lock, was looking straight back at her with a pleased smile. The steaming pot was before them – Janice smiled back at her old school friend as she began pouring the tea.

'Well, you did it, Janice. You really did it this time. Now you're in your dream cottage, a few days before the big three zero,' said Sandy. Her voluminous retro chic pixie curls gave her a striking appearance.

'Yes, thirty in a few days.' Janice raised a happy eyebrow.

'And what does your Simon think of it all?'

'I think Simon will enjoy the New Forest way of life too. I'm sure we both will, Sandy. It's already a picture of utter winter glee.' Janice looked out of the kitchen window into the snow-covered garden. 'I never thought I'd enjoy the winter like this. Our ideal little isolated cottage with New Forest trees and heathland in abundance. Simon loves it. He's out now, walking the dog through the woods to the side of the place. During the week, he does it of a morning before work and again when he comes home. He takes a torch with him.'

Sandy's big brown eyes widened with mock surprise upon her attractive Caribbean and Caucasian mixed-race features. Her brows raised and touched her cascading curls. She had a fetching and enthusiastic grin. 'Oh, that wood comes out onto open heathland. That should look nice in the snow. Upon the top of the heath, there's another small section of woodland. The late Mr Ballantyne used to call that place the Little Wood.'

Janice blew into her hot tea. 'Mr Ballantyne's son spoke of his father's love of the place when we were buying the cottage. He said his father's body was found in the Little Wood. He went to some lengths to tell us how his father was drawn to the place. Even visiting the woods on his final moment – he sat down and passed away with a peaceful smile on his face, so I was told.'

Sandy nodded and looked into her teacup. She was pondering the late Mr Ballantyne. 'He was a very odd, but kindly man. He was into Wicca and that sort of thing – believed in forest spirits and all. He corresponded with witches all over the world – an occultist by all accounts. Devoted to Witchcraft and all that sort of tommyrot.'

Janice laughed. 'Simon heard something about that from a couple of New Age type travellers a few days ago. He thought they were just old weirdos being weird. You know what he's like with trendy lefties,' replied Janice.

Sandy giggled. 'Is that what Simon calls such people? I'm not surprised. He doesn't suffer certain types gladly. New Age hippies must be right up there with the trendy left-wing politicos. I think I know the very people you mean.'

Janice laughed and agreed. 'In Simon's rather narrowed perspective. He was polite with the old New Agers but he takes no notice of most left-leaning types. These people told Simon they got along with the late Mr Ballantyne because of his Wiccan beliefs. They found the old man very interesting.'

'Yes,' said Sandy, 'and your Simon is just a little too right-leaning for such conversation?'

'Yes,' agreed Janice. Then she added, 'A little to the right of Genghis Khan.'

They both sipped their tea and then Sandy put her hand to her mouth as though she might supress the laughter. She could imagine Simon trying to contain himself and be polite.

'Oh, I'm sure Simon's eye was twitching the way it normally does when he can't see eye to eye with someone. I can see your Simon trying to smile while not believing or respecting a word of what was being said to him,' Sandy said, laughing.

Janice sighed and looked up as she shook her head. 'Oh, he had a few choice things to say about the New Age couple once he came in with Nelly. They were parked just outside, in the gravel passing place, beyond the Side Wood. Also, we nearly bumped into them again when taking Nelly for her walk yesterday. We made a none too subtle about-turn and walked the other way. The lady seemed like a nice person to me, like an over-aged hippy who never got off the bus. I'm sure there's no harm in the eccentric couple from my own point of view. The woman remained sitting in the old people carrier she drives – her partner or husband got out and went up the heath to the Little Wood again. They definitely seem to have a fascination with the place.'

'They live in Ringwood,' added Sandy.

'Really? So, they drove that old people carrier through the snow from Ringwood to visit the Little Wood? All for the memory of Mr Ballantyne? That is kind.

'According to Simon, the woman had some Wiccan thing the first time he saw them. She told him she'd put it up in the Little Wood where Mr Ballantyne was found dead, back in mid-August. Evidently, they also said the late Mr Ballantyne had a serene smile upon his face as his son had told us. Simon also told me these New Agers remarked on Mr Ballantyne being completely at peace with himself and the world when his body was found. Then the woman added that the old man must have seen the little folk. I'm not sure what was meant by that, but Simon politely nodded and moved on. He was probably a little rude, I can't say for sure. But you know as well as I—'

'Simon will not suffer fools gladly,' Sandy interrupted with a giggle.

'Got it in one,' agreed Janice, then she continued, 'At the time, these old hippies got back in their battered old people carrier and left. No doubt, Simon probably muttered a few of his colourful expletives once the van moved off. I'm sure you can well imagine what he might have said. Anyway, when we saw the weird couple again yesterday, Simon wanted to avoid them. Therefore, we took Nelly for a walk in the other direction.'

Sandy lifted her teacup with both hands and raised an amused eyebrow. 'I always said hello to Mr Ballantyne if I bumped into him in Lymington, then I'd make my excuses as quick as possible to leave. He believed in all sorts of impish forest spirits and could be a little fanciful. It was probably the late Mr Ballantyne who put the little folk idea to the "over the hill" New Agers. They were probably joking about the old man's eccentricities when they spoke to Simon. They're rather laid-back and humorous once you get to know them. Their names are Abigail and Raymond. I once told Mr Ballantyne about Abigail and her Wiccan ways – I might have set Mr Ballantyne off with his friendship towards the chalk and cheese couple.'

'So, you know the New Age couple to talk to?' asked Janice.

'I knew of them by sight before I ever spoke to them. Then I began to have the odd chat with Abigail Chalkley concerning Mr Ballantyne. I've since chatted to them on a number of occasions, often in the local supermarket in Lymington. Just small talk, nothing more. They seem to get on with most people in the town. They're sort of regular faces that everyone knows,' said Sandy.

'I presume you also came across Mr Ballantyne pottering about town too?' asked Janice.

'Yes, I did. Very often, in fact. On one occasion when I spoke with Abigail and Raymond, in the supermarket, Mr Ballantyne was with them. I suppose that's how I got better acquainted with them. The old man stopped me in the shopping aisle by the bread counter – the New Age couple were with him. We would always nod and acknowledge one another after that.'

'Oh, so you became acquainted with the New Age couple because of you knowing Mr Ballantyne?' added Janice.

'Yes, I suppose I did. I got to know Mr Ballantyne because he came to our practice once. He wasn't my patient but we all knew him from the waiting room. He chatted to everyone.'

'About his strange beliefs?' Janice asked.

'Yes, Mr Ballantyne would always be trying to convince people of his beliefs. He was politely shunned by the final year of his life – people felt sorry for him and thought he was suffering from some form of dementia. I'm not sure this was so. He seemed astute, but he spoke of such far-fetched folklore. I think this came about from his Wiccan faith. It is, after all, a weird and bizarre cult. I would imagine that New Age people would find him interesting. I also think he believed what he was saying. The Little Wood does have a rather spooky feel to it. I'm sure the imagination can work overtime if one is lonely and inclined to such beliefs. He lived here all alone and often went up there to the Little Wood. Daily, I believe. He was obsessed with the Little Wood by all accounts, completely devoted to it and the imagined impish beings that, he believed, lived there. He would always try to talk of such mischievous beings to me. I'd make a polite excuse to leave, but he would always call his warning after me: "Never let them kiss you."'

Janice smiled sympathetically. 'I know, bless the poor old man. His son spoke of such things too. To use his son's exact words, "drifting off the rails" was how he described his dear old dad.'

'Off the rails is rather playing it down,' Sandy replied.

Janice giggled and put her hand to her mouth. 'I mustn't speak ill of poor Mr Ballantyne.'

'What else did his son speak of?' Sandy asked. She was inquisitive about the old man, even though she avoided chatting to him when he was alive.

Janice stopped sniggering and looked directly back at Sandy. 'So, you have experienced some of these rumoured things about the late Mr Ballantyne when he was alive?'

'Of course, I'm wondering if his son told you what the old man tried to discuss with me and many other locals,' replied Sandy. 'Poor Mr Ballantyne seemed convinced. Everyone began to give him a wide birth over such tales.'

Janice retained the amused smirk. 'What? About waking strange Wiccan forces in *the Little Wood*? And strange little impish creatures? Yet you maintain that he wasn't going crazy?'

Sandy sighed. 'His talk was outlandish, but Mr Ballantyne genuinely believed his Wiccan

things. The man was devoted. I think he was ostra-
cised from other Wiccan groups. Only those two
New Agers indulged him towards the end. I think
they felt sorry for him.'

'So, their friendship towards him was more for
pity? Not the shared Wiccan beliefs?' Janice asked.

'I'm certain that those old New Age people took
Mr Ballantyne seriously, even if they didn't believe
his tales. What little I could work out about them
was their fondness and respect for the man.

'When Abigail and Raymond say little folk, they
actually mean fairies,' Sandy said, laughing. 'They
know Mr Ballantyne really believed such things
and I think Abigail and Raymond just payed polite
lip service. Our New Age friends wouldn't likely
believe in celestial creatures too. I would have
thought Druids, witches and trees are their thing.
The wraith-like things are the reason why everyone
avoided the poor old man towards the end of his
life.'

'Except for Abigail and Raymond, these "wan-
nabe" converts.' Janice chuckled as she drank some
more tea.

'They live in their little world of make-believe,'
added Sandy. 'Harmless, like Mr Ballantyne, but
still people to keep at arm's length in my opinion.
Yet I don't think they believed Mr Ballantyne. I
think they felt sorry for him. Also, they shared some

Wiccan interests – he was into spells and things. I'm certain Abigail is too.'

'Is she a witch?' Janice asked thoughtfully.

'I wouldn't be surprised if she practised such things. She embraces the New Age and Wiccan ideology from what I gather. It's what they had in common,' replied Sandy.

Again, Janice nodded. 'Yes, his son said as much. They flirted with the notion of putting the old man in a home, but his son decided against it because Mr Ballantyne wouldn't have wanted such a thing. His son said his father seemed to have all his faculties apart from this strange fixation with the existence of fairies. Evidently, the old man was insistent in his claim to have seen such creatures. He even had a spell to protect him from becoming bewitched by them. He regarded himself as a guardian of the Little Wood.'

'Yes,' Sandy put her hand over her mouth and continued to giggle, 'I'm afraid this was so. His spell was probably one of his many Wiccan fantasies. Maybe something Abigail and Raymond, the New Agers, helped concoct. Poor old Mr Ballantyne seemed obsessed by fairies in his final years. I wouldn't be surprised if Abigail and Raymond indulged him with the spell – if he believed it worked then all the better. He was a sweet old man with this strange imagination. Most of his eccentric

Wiccan studies were easily tolerated but the belief of fairies was taking things a tad too far. Indeed, it could be said that Mr Ballantyne was quite literally, away with the fairies.'

'Not literally, Sandy,' Janice laughed, 'literally would imply they are real.'

'Oh!' Sandy burst into laughter. 'Sorry, not literally speaking then. That's pushing the issue too far.'

The two ladies chuckled over the strange story of the late Mr Ballantyne. It was a natural thing to do and often the way of people during private chit-chat. They went on to discuss other things as the pleasant morning drifted towards the afternoon.

CHAPTER 4

SANDY STOPS OFF IN LYMINGTON

Sandy thought it had been a very pleasant after-noon indeed as she drove carefully along the snowy forest road towards Lymington. Thankfully, the gritters had been out. This had helped a little but the drive was still slower than usual because Sandy was a naturally cautious person. The day was overcast and the forest added to the dull day.

Her car's Bluetooth device started to flash and ring and she saw her husband's name light up on the small screen. She pressed the button to answer. 'I'm on my way home, Harry,' she said, knowing he was making sure all was well.

'Oh good,' replied Harry's crackled voice. 'I think we're in for another heavy flurry soon.'

She sighed as she cautiously steered the white Range Rover along the sludgy forest road. 'I thought as much. There are still a few hours before dusk. I'm stopping off in Lymington to get a few things. Do you want anything?'

'Can you get some white pepper and horseradish sauce please? I've done a nice beef roast. I bought a joint in town today, but I forgot how low we were on white pepper and horseradish sauce.'

Sandy laughed as she replied, 'We mustn't forget the horseradish sauce. I'm going to get a bottle of that French claret from the supermarket. Do you want any beers?'

'No thanks. However, I would like some of that claret too,' he replied with a chuckle.

Then in unison, Sandy and Harry both added, 'We better get two bottles.'

They both laughed as the dark foliage vanished and the grey sky appeared – Sandy suddenly entered Lymington town. She quickly added, 'I'll be about twenty minutes.'

'See you in twenty – love you!'

'Love you too,' she replied and turned the Bluetooth off. She spotted a parking space along the main road and quickly pulled in behind an old worn Toyota Townace – a metallic grey people carrier. She instantly recognised the vehicle. It was Abigail's and Raymond's old run around – the New Agers were in Lymington.

As Sandy got out, she saw Abigail coming along the pavement towards her people carrier. The middle-aged woman was wearing her usual long rainbow-patterned cardigan, the garish garment hanging down past her knees. Underneath, she wore a thick, terracotta roll-neck jumper with purple low-crotch harem trousers. All uncomplemented by thick-soled sand boots. A worried expression peered out from long straggly hair with an unfashionable purple-dyed streak down one side. Her cold, red nose poked out upon a red-cheeked face. The majority of the uncoloured hair was brown with the odd strands of wispy grey making her look the complete old latter-day Hippie. She was holding a carrier bag to her chest with both arms around it, her van keys clasped in one hand while pressed against the shopping bag. Her look was distant and lost, consumed with concern. Oblivious to everything around her.

'Abigail,' called Sandy as she stood in the woman's path.

Abigail snapped out of her worried daydream. She recognised Sandy and knew she had spoken with her on odd occasions. Small talk, nothing more. She knew Sandy was a local face, one who knew the late Mr Ballantyne.

'Please don't think me intrusive, Abigail, but you look very concerned. Are you alright?' Sandy asked as she pointed her car key at the Range Rover and clicked the lock on.

Abigail was not surprised Sandy knew her by name, even though she couldn't recall giving it during their minor small talks. But then many people knew her and Raymond, even people they'd never spoken with.

'Oh, hello,' Abigail replied politely. Her voice was strained. 'I'm sorry, I was miles away.'

'Oh, that's alright,' replied Sandy. 'You seemed awfully worried. I just wondered if you were OK? Where's Raymond?'

'He's in hospital,' replied Abigail. 'I'm just going there now. I've bought him a few things.' She looked into the bag she was holding.

'Oh, I'm so sorry, Abigail. I do hope it's not serious?'

'Have you not heard?' Abigail replied, realising that Sandy didn't know of her recent circumstance.

Sandy looked a little perplexed. 'I've not heard of anything.'

Abigail took a deep breath and then it all came pouring out. 'I'm afraid it's very serious indeed. Raymond has had some strange type of breakdown. A really bad one. This is something completely out of character for him. It's all happened in a very short space of time.'

Sandy frowned in disbelief. 'Raymond's had a breakdown? When did this happen?'

'This time yesterday, everything was fine. I was driving us here to Lymington. We were on the road that passes the Little Wood and Raymond had been going on about leaving a lock knife up by a tree where we'd put up a spiritual ornament for Mr Ballantyne a day earlier. Raymond had been absent-minded and left his lock knife there. As we were passing the very place, he asked me to stop the van so he could go up the heathland, to the Little Wood and look for it. I parked and waited while he went up to the woods. He was gone for quite some time while I was sitting in the van with the engine running to keep warm. I saw the new people from the cottage come out with their black Labrador and they walked the other way. After a while, I decided to get out and go up to the Little Wood because Raymond was taking so long. I met him staggering down the path as the snow started to fall. He was totally stressed out – completely in a mental mess and muttering to himself. I don't know what happened and I couldn't get any sense from him. He just kept blabbering that we must never go to the Little Wood again. He was running from something he saw.'

'Oh my God! This is terrible, Abigail. Did he not compose himself afterwards?' asked Sandy.

Abigail shook her head and looked at Sandy. 'He got worse. We got into the van and carried on our way here to Lymington. All the way he was blabbering nervously about wicked little things – I couldn't get any sense out of him. When we got here and out of the van he started ranting and making a spectacle of himself. Right here, in this very street! It was awful and people all about the place were looking at us. I was trying to calm him down but he was just shouting at everyone, calling them unbelievers and that the only way to stay safe was to never let them kiss you. "One kiss and that is it!" He kept repeating it: "One kiss and that is it!" Some people tried to help me calm him down, then a police car arrived and as they tried to talk him down, he backed away into a shop doorway. He was pleading with the policemen to believe him. He was in tears and beside himself with this strange type of grief as he tried to convince the policemen…'

'Convince the policemen of what?' Sandy gently coaxed her to continue.

Abigail sighed. 'That there were little impish things in the Little Wood and they could transfix anyone who looked at them. He called to me and implored me to believe that Mr Ballantyne was right all along and that he needed the spell in my old book.'

'A spell from your old book?' whispered Sandy. She was most intrigued. Abigail was not hysterical or being neurotic, she was clearly confused and concerned, yet she was carefully explaining Raymond's bizarre state of mind.

'Yes, I have a book of Wiccan spells. An indulgent interest for the most part. Raymond was suddenly imploring me to take a particular spell seriously, one I'd used as an indulgence once before – with the late Mr Ballantyne.'

Sandy was shocked by Abigail's revelation. Not so much by the book but by Raymond's strange behaviour. 'Then what happened?'

'As one policeman tried to approach him, Raymond pulled out the lock knife he had retrieved earlier from the Little Wood. He cut his wrist before our eyes. There was this ghastly fountain of blood – it seemed to shoot everywhere. The two policemen had to do a great deal of emergency procedure to abate further loss before the ambulance arrived. At first, they had to wrestle with Raymond in order to keep him down. I think he quickly lost strength – they had the help of a passing off-duty paramedic too. It was all so frightening. I was useless, just standing there beside myself with terror.'

'Oh my God, Abigail. This is so awful. I'm so sorry. Is there anything I can do for you?'

'Not at the moment, thank you. I think Raymond is heavily sedated and there are doctors doing tests. There are also psychic evaluators. At least, that's what I think they're called. Raymond is on suicide watch, but even when he comes out of his sleep, tired and exhausted, he's still trying to convince me that the Little Wood is dangerous. He's insisting that he needs this mystical magic spell. He keeps going on about the one I used on the late Mr Ballantyne. He thought it was a complete joke before, something that worked on a troubled mind. A placebo effect he was happy to indulge the old man with. Raymond was fond of the eccentric old boy. Now he's saying Mr Ballantyne was right about the spell in my book of Wiccan things, insisting that Mr Ballantyne was right about the little fairies too. The silly ritual thing I did from my old book some years ago was all proper and correct. Now Raymond needs the same spell too.'

'Perhaps Raymond is hoping that the same placebo effect will compel him to be better? The same way it worked for Mr Ballantyne?' Sandy frowned while she nodded.

'I just concocted a potion with lemon balm and a few other elementary herbs, then I read out this small verse from an old book of Wiccan spells. It's just a well-meaning ritual. It's not real, I just did it because I thought Mr Ballantyne believed it would work. I was indulging the old man. He once went through an episode similar to this – we discovered him in a wretched emotional state on one occasion when we visited him.'

'Mr Ballantyne was in exactly the same state?' Sandy asked in a low voice. She found the tale incredible.

Abigail nodded and replied, 'Yes. Raymond and I reasoned that if Mr Ballantyne believed the spell, then perhaps he might level out a little. I know it sounds utterly pathetic but it actually worked for Mr Ballantyne. He still insisted that the fairies were real, but he argued they could no longer kiss him – that he'd no longer be smitten by the diabolical kiss of these wraith-like things. He completely calmed down.'

'I see,' Sandy looked thoughtful, 'so your spell had a psychological effect and Raymond is clasping at the same straw?'

'I think so. In private, Raymond and I insisted it was nothing more than a silly placebo effect. But now Raymond is insisting that there are little semi-naked wraith-like people running about the woods too. He says Mr Ballantyne was right and the spell could work for him too. Like Mr Ballantyne, Raymond is insisting that flowers grow and bloom instantly in the presence of these wraith-like things. Leaves on trees grow in seconds and when these giggling creatures walk away these flowers and leaves quickly wither and die. How could he think silly things like this up?'

'I'm so sorry, Abigail. This all sounds dreadful,' replied Sandy. She slowly shook her head in disbelief. The torment on Abigail's face was apparent for all to see.

Abigail looked back towards the mini supermarket and added, 'I'm surprised the shop people served me after what happened yesterday.'

'I'm sure they know you're going through a very stressful time,' Sandy added comfortingly.

Then Abigail pointed at a small shop's doorway. 'It happed just there. The snowfall has covered the blood. It was everywhere.'

'I do hope Raymond gets better, Abigail. I'm so sorry to hear this. If there is anything I can do, please let me know.' She handed Abigail a small card with her number on it.

Abigail took the card while still holding the shopping bag. She pressed her keys and the van's locks clicked. She managed to pull the sliding door open and place the shopping inside, then she took a moment to look at the card Sandy had given her. She read the name: Sandy Lock, consultant psychiatrist – along with a mobile number, a landline and an email.

'You're a qualified mental health consultant?' She turned back to look at Sandy.

'Yes, I can help Raymond and you,' replied Sandy.

'That is most decent and I thank you for that kindness,' she said, smiling.

Sandy looked past Abigail into the van. Upon the seat was a tattered-looking book. 'Is that the book you were speaking of?'

Abigail sighed. 'Yes, it is. I know it sounds utterly pathetic, but I'm prepared to read the spell out to him. After all, if it doesn't work, it won't make him any worse. I'm going for the psychological shot – it's the only thing I know I can try.'

Sandy read the title out, '*Witchcraft – Spells and Potions* by Matilda Hoskins. That is a rather old book, Abigail.'

'I don't think it's as old as it looks, lady. It's just a bit tatty. I've heard that the woman was from these parts – there are local people who remember her,' she replied, then stared nervously at Sandy.

Sandy's face showed deep concern but she managed a kindly smile, it was the way of her profession. 'One never knows and it certainly can't do any harm, especially if you're reading it to someone who's convinced it will work. Just out of interest, how did you come across this book?'

'Well, lady, I bought it in Brockenhurst about eight years ago. It was in an old book shop,' she replied.

Sandy stepped forward and put her hand gently and reassuringly on Abigail's arm. 'Please call me Sandy. I can help you. I would like to help. May I have your number too?'

'Y-yes of course you can, Sandy. I would like that,' replied Abigail anxiously. She Bluetoothed her number and seemed well adept with her mobile phone.

Sandy immediately got the message on her device and began to type Abigail into her contacts.

'Thank you, I'll phone later in the evening after you've visited Raymond. Would that be alright?'

Abigail smiled timidly. 'Oh yes, Sandy, that would be rather kind of you. I'd appreciate that very much.'

She smiled. 'I give you my word, Abigail, I will phone you. I'd like to if it's not intrusive.'

'It's not intrusive, Sandy. Thank you.' Abigail smiled and turned away.

Sandy lingered and watched as Abigail slid the side door of the van shut. The ungainly woman then walked around to the driver's side and awkwardly got into the van. She started the vehicle and then pulled out onto the main road to drive off. There was a desperate look about her. A clarity of the dilemma Abigail was in.

Sandy watched as the people carrier turned a corner. She was standing in stunned disbelief. Raymond must have been saying the same things to Abigail as the late Mr Ballantyne had often said to her. She whispered the words to herself, 'Never let them kiss you.'

She inhaled the cold winter's air and then released a warm vapour of breath, the steam visible like a small fog in the cold evening street. Then she proceeded towards the mini supermarket. There'd be a few things to talk to Harry about over dinner when she got home.

CHAPTER 5

A FINISHED PROJECT AND
THE DOG WALK

It was later in the afternoon. Sandy had gone home and Janice was putting a bottle of red wine with two glasses upon a tray. She went to the cellar stairs and carefully descended. In the basement, Simon stood before the small doll's house he had finally completed for his niece. He looked up at her.

'Steady as you go,' he said, laughing.

'I am,' she replied with a broad grin. She made her way to the table by the doll's house and put the tray down. She turned and looked at Simon's finished project.

'So, you've finished,' she said, thrilled. 'Oh Simon! You've surpassed yourself. It looks wonderful.'

'Oh, yes indeed! I like these compliments. They make my head swell. Keep them coming, don't be bashful.' He was delighted with his completed project. The pretty doll's house looked resplendent as it bathed in the shafts of daylight that came through the tiny cellar window on the upper part of the wall.

Simon sighed, feeling most gratified. 'I'm glad I put off the final touches until we moved in.'

Janice nodded. 'I agree, it looks so cute.'

'Could any little girl want more?' he asked with a teasing grin.

'I don't think so,' replied Janice. 'We've been here just two weeks and you've finished Vicky's doll's house. Now that little bee is out of your bonnet we can look forward to new undertakings.' She poured the red wine into each glass.

Simon took his wine and raised it. 'To new ventures and our glorious little abode in the New Forest. I've dreamed of this ever since that weekend when you showed me Beaulieu and we stayed at that Bed and Breakfast. Now we're living the dream.'

'I know, darling, you've told me on a number of occasions.' She smiled and then whispered, 'I don't like to think back to that particular time.'

'We had a wonderful long weekend…' He stopped realising that she was feeling guilty about the infidelity to her ex-husband. 'Are you still thinking of Frank? You made your choice and what's done, is done.'

She put her wine down. 'Oh, I know, Simon, but I can't help feeling bad at my betrayal. I tried to justify what I did at the time. I just feel a little sorry for him now. I hope he finds someone who will make him happy.'

'He never knew we were having an affair during the marriage, so why worry when he has no idea he'd been a cuckold? You had both drifted apart long before I came along.' He put his arm around her and pulled her to his side then placed his forehead down upon hers and looked into her raised blue eyes. 'We have no need to worry about these things anymore, Angel. It's just you and me now in our little isolated cottage. I have my job in Southampton and you're now working in Lymington. We've got jam on it, girl.' He laughed in his usual roguish manner – one of his more carefree ways she'd found attractive.

She smiled and couldn't help wondering how she had ever fallen for him. A rough and ready man from East London's Bow district. Not to her tastes at all, normally. Yet he had something about him that excited her. So much so, she'd craftily instigated the situation to begin the affair with him. Janice had told Simon she was in the process of getting divorced when she wasn't. She had been flirting with the idea. She flirted with lots of ideas.

Fortunately, Simon had risen to the bait. He was egged on by her attentions. Soon they had unashamedly started a tempestuous affair, a fraught situation of excitement and clashing egos. Eventually, they seemed to find a happy medium. Where? Neither could say. They just emerged from the storm of passionate excitement and drifted with the new and gentle flow of things.

With her former husband Frank, Janice had ruled the roost and was used to getting her own way. Simon, however, was a different type of man entirely. He had met her head-on when she tried to sculpture him to her wants, or what she had perceived to be her image of him. To her surprise he had resisted her stubbornly and often came back at her, verbally fighting with conviction and confidence. His tongue was as sharp as hers and he knew when to deliver a counter knock-back.

She begrudgingly admired this aspect of him, though on occasions he could be too stubborn and she had learned to be more subtle when trying to make a point. Janice had modified and often changed her approach.

Simon had quickly caught on to this adaptation and was always on his guard. Sometimes it was a comical thing to observe, on other occasions it could be exasperating. This was because Simon would be suspicious over small things that she regarded as irrelevant.

She took another sip of wine and smiled to herself remembering some of their arguments.

Simon frowned. 'What's on your mind, Little Bean? You have that dirty "Devil may care" look! The one you wear when you're thinking up some sly scheme. One to put on me.'

Again, she giggled and almost choked on her wine, coughing and spluttering between laughs. She dropped the glass on the floor. It shattered spilling the red wine across the stone, while Simon playfully wrestled with her as she continued to laugh.

'Come on, Little Bean, tell me what ghastly little thing is on your mind.' He lifted her onto the work bench so she was sitting. He pressed his way between her open legs with his arms about her waist and kissed her passionately. His eyes suddenly widened as he broke away from his embracing kiss.

'I've realised what you were saying before. You little minx. You just tried to glimmer me.' He grinned at her like he'd uncovered some devious ploy.

'Glimmer you? What on earth do you mean?' she countered and giggled. Janice had other schemes on her mind, but not at that precise moment.

Simon closed his eyes mockingly, playfully suspicious of a devious plan. 'You have something else on your mind. No time to let dust settle.'

'Simon, are you on one of your conspiracy theory jaunts?'

'Oh, now I know what you mean by "new undertakings". There is a ghastly little something you have

planned and the wine is a way of saying, "You've finished that, now I'll point you in a new direction."'
He stepped back with his tongue against his bottom lip as he tried to fathom her out. Suddenly, he was on his guard.

'No, I'm not.' She laughed. He was of course correct, but Janice would never admit to such a thing.

'God, you little minx. I'm being buttered up, aren't I?'

'No,' she laughed again, 'you're so suspicious.'

'I've learned to be on my guard around you. It's become second nature.'

Janice smiled and shook her head. She stared at him intently and lied, 'Well, there's no need to be.'

He looked at his fine doll's house and changed the subject. 'What do you think?'

Janice looked at it and replied quietly. 'I think it's absolutely adorable. Any little girl would love such a thing – your niece will be thrilled with it. We've already covered this ground.'

He sighed and looked up through the high cellar window and shivered. 'I'll be glad when January's gone. Only a couple of days left now.'

'Why? February will still be cold.' She was beginning to feel playful, but contained herself, conscious he was having a contemplative moment. She'd indulge him, knowing he always came out of such minor dispositions feeling happy and game for her attentions.

'We will only have February to go. After that, the spring will come.'

'The weather forecast had predicted more snow. I never thought it would be so heavy,' she said, looking up at the basement window where the snow was piling against the lower pane.

'I want to see the place in spring,' added Simon enthusiastically.

'It isn't too bad now – I love seeing the New Forest in snow,' Janice replied.

'We'll take Nelly out for another walk in it. She loves the place. I don't think she'd ever seen snow until we moved here,' said Simon.

An excited bark came from up the cellar stairs as the patter of paws was heard. Suddenly, Nelly, the black Labrador, scrambled down the steps excitedly. She was wagging her tail and jumping up at them. The lovable mutt whined and barked eagerly.

'Where did she come from?' Simon said, laughing.

Janice took another sip of wine from Simon's glass. 'She was in the kitchen in her basket, sleeping.'

'Until she heard her name and the magic word,' he added.

'Oh, the magic word,' she muttered.

'Don't say it or she'll raise the needle on the potty-dog-ometer,' whispered Simon.

'What "WALK!" Do you mean that word?'

Nelly began yelping and whining with added vigour, unable to contain her excitement. She jumped up at Simon knowing he was the one who did the walks, while Janice always said the magic word.

'Aw! I knew you was going to say that. You said it on purpose.' He pursed his lips in mock annoyance.

'I couldn't resist it,' she replied with a look of glee in her mischievous eyes.

He looked down at the boisterous Nelly. 'Go get your lead then, girl.'

Nelly yelped again and sped off up the cellar stairs, while Janice and Simon chuckled at the dog's antics. They could hear her crashing around in the open kitchen cupboard where the lead was kept on the wooden floor. In a moment, the lovable dog was bounding down the stairs with the item in her mouth, shaking her bottom and wagging her tail like a dancing banshee.

'Alright then, you soppy old mutt. I'll get my coat,' said Simon.

'Wait for me,' called Janice as she jumped off the work bench. 'I'm coming too.'

In moments, they were closing the cottage door and Nelly was bounding off along the footpath that led into the woodland at the side of the cottage. A copse of trees Janice and Simon had christened the Side Wood.

Nelly's lead was now a symbol of going for walks. They never put the lovable mutt on the tether when walking through the Side Wood, only if they were walking along the lane. The black Labrador had developed a keen road sense – she was aware of traffic, roads and kerbs. Nelly also knew the woodlands were areas where restraint and tolerance were different from town walks.

As Janice stepped onto the snow-covered path, a fresh flurry began to fall, much to her delight.

'Hey, we timed that well,' she said.

'Do you think it will create another lay?' asked Simon, looking up into the fresh falling snow.

'Hopefully,' she replied as they made their way along the path and into the Side Wood, where Nelly had shot off along the trail she had come to know so well over the past few days.

Janice breathed in the cold air. 'Do you think the wood has a fairy tale splendour in the snow?'

'Yes,' Simon agreed. 'Like something from those old German and Danish fairy tale writers.'

Janice nodded. 'The Brothers Grimm and Hans Christian Andersen. Yes, it has that mystical feel.'

They both watched as the white flurry began to filter down through the barren branches, beautiful white droplets floating down against the dark background of the clustered trees.

'Can you smell the ferns?' she asked.

'Yes, it's a lovely scent. A fresh and clean aroma. Ultra-invigorating,' he replied.

'Ultra?' Janice said delightedly. 'You must be impressed.'

He grinned. 'I am. I think it excites Nelly so much more. Dogs have a sharper sense of smell then we do. Every smell is amplified and must be wonderfully interesting.'

Janice looked around at the beauty of the snow-covered woodland and the white New Forest floor.

'It's absolutely gorgeous.' She looked up more intently, and observed snowflakes and shafts of light penetrating the upper branches and twigs.

'No leaves left to stop the snow getting through the woodland's branches to the forest floor. It must be getting heavier,' she said.

'We'll see when we get to the heathland. That leads to the Little Wood. We haven't gone to the top of the heath yet, perhaps we should today. It's about time we took a peek.' He remained enchanted while observing the snowflakes coming through the branches.

'Yes, we finally get to visit the copse of trees where Mr Ballantyne often went to ponder,' she added.

'Yes, without his son or weird New Agers doing their silly Wiccan and fairy nonsense.' He looked up through the branches.

'The sky is getting greyer. Perhaps it's the bare branches that make it so,' she said.

'I think you're right. I believe it is getting heavier.' Simon looked down and smiled at her.

'The smell of the ferns is much stronger than I could ever have imagined,' Janice said, looking around.

Simon agreed. 'A strong smell – almost like pine, but a little sweeter.'

'It's a wonderful clean smell.'

'Pure nature – uncorrupted and non-polluted,' he added, looking about him and allowing the chill to sweep through his body – a soothing yet uncanny thing. 'I'm wondering if it's another type of smell, mixed in with the pine.'

'Hey, look at this,' called Janice as she walked over to a tree.

'What is it?' asked Simon.

'This branch still has leaves on it,' she replied.

Simon stood next to her. He looked all over the tree. Its branches were bare of leaves as one would expect in mid-winter. All over, apart from a small lower branch that had vibrant green leaves like it was in mid-summer bloom. He frowned and then before their very eyes the leaves began to quickly wither and die, each brown and withered dead leaf breaking and falling to the snowy floor.

'Have you ever seen anything like this?' he asked.

'Never,' Janice replied.

Suddenly, Nelly began to bark. Simon and Janice looked to the mutt. They could see a trail of vibrant green-leafed patches on trees and bushes. The foliage had suddenly appeared. Then, as sudden as it appeared, the greenery started withering and dying in the same uncanny manner, small clumps of sporadic, rotting flora dropping into the winter snow.

'It's eerie,' muttered Simon.

'I don't know anything about plants, but I've never heard anyone talk of such a thing. This is winter and we're looking at foliage that blooms the way it does in summer then withers and dies in an instant,' Janice said as she looked around at the small patches of foliage withering and rotting before their eyes.

'A section of tree or shrub blooming and rotting in seconds,' added Simon.

'Maybe it's a particular thing to these forest plants. I never knew of such a thing, but then I'm not up on forest or plant life,' Janice concluded.

'Me neither. But I think you must be right. Perhaps it's unique to some types of forest plants. Holly is green in winter,' Simon suggested.

'It's bloody creepy though.' Janice looked up and about the bare trees – there was no foliage higher up. She looked back down and all signs of the recently green patches of foliage were gone.

'One moment it was there. The next, gone,' said Simon in bemused fascination.

'How do you explain that?' she asked.

'I can't. But look! There are small footprints in the snow here, next to the decaying flora,' said Simon.

'The footprints are bare feet. Little tiny feet like those of a small child.' Janice was perplexed.

Simon looked about. 'I hope this isn't some bloody hoax. The sort of things tricksters like to do, in order to cause conspiracy and what not. I wouldn't put it past those weird blooming New Agers to concoct something like this. That blooming fella of hers was outside of the people carrier yesterday, when we saw her sitting there with the bloody engine running. Those weirdos seem to have a fascination with the place. They're not the full shilling, I'm telling you, Jan. Something's blooming weird about them.'

'This whole bloody place is peculiar. I've never seen anything like this,' said Janice.

Simon suddenly adopted a more pragmatic approach. 'Perhaps there's a whole host of strange things we need to get used to. Remember, we are city kids, like your old school friend Sandy. She got used to it. We've moved away from the big city into a more natural environment. I bet Sandy knows of such things.'

'She's a city girl too,' replied Janice.

'I know, but she moved out here five years back. I bet she knows a few things more than us, especially about the overall New Forest area,' he added.

'This is the Side Wood next to our house. We've not even got to the Little Wood yet. That's supposed to be the weird place,' Janice said, laughing.

CHAPTER 6

SANDY AND HARRY'S
DINING ROOM CHAT

Sandy poured a refill into her husband's wine glass. They had finished their rather splendid beef roast and each felt content with their evening repast. Harry smiled his thanks, his long face beaming with pleasure and his pale-blue eyes shining beneath wavy gold hair. He was a strikingly handsome man in Sandy's eyes. Also, kind and engaging when together. He seemed to be able to talk about most things.

'I do like your beef roasts,' said Sandy as she started to refill her own wine glass.

'I know. That's why I thought I might get one cooked for you,' replied Harry as he lifted his wine glass to her.

'In all, it's been a rather interesting day, to say the least.' Sandy took a sip of her wine.

'It certainly seems like a strange thing you've experienced. Especially the thing with Abigail and her partner Raymond. I know the couple you mean, but I only know of them by sight. I've never spoken to them. I never really spoke to old Mr Ballantyne either, though I can remember him well. It's strange, there are so many people I know by sight, but I've never spoken to them. Regular people I've known since I was a child. I suppose there are a few who know me by sight despite us never having spoken.'

'You're a New Forest person through and through. Are any of these people I speak of like you? Born and raised here?' Sandy asked.

'Old Mr Ballantyne was. The New Age couple have been about for around twelve or fifteen years, I think. I don't know where they're from originally.'

'The woman, Abigail, was awfully upset about her partner Raymond. She seemed quite lost.'

Harry nodded. 'I can imagine she would feel this way. It must have been very traumatic for all who saw that happen in the main street.'

Sandy was slowly turning her wine glass while looking into the red wine. 'The retro New Agers were among the few who seemed to indulge Mr Ballantyne and his strange ways. Did you know that Abigail even conjured a Wiccan-style spell from an old spell book she had? She never believed the spell, but it was an indulgence for the late Mr Ballantyne. He seemed to believe it. At least, that's what I'm guessing.'

Harry chuckled. 'Retro New Agers! I like that. This Abigail probably thought she was doing the old man a favour from a psychological point of view. A bit like an exorcist in the Roman Catholic church. I've heard that they are more for the psychological approach as opposed to the real belief of celestial demons and things. If they can convince a troubled mind that something is wrong and they have the cure, it could have a placebo effect. The troubled mind believes and, in effect, cures itself.'

Sandy smiled and then chuckled. 'So, Abigail might be a Wiccan exorcist but doesn't know it?'

Harry raised an eyebrow and added, 'Perhaps, from the late Mr Ballantyne's point of view.'

'Yet from Abigail's, an accidental benefit. You might have struck a point with that little theory. A psychological exorcist for the believers of paranormal things.' Sandy turned the thought over in her mind.

'I'm sure Raymond's affliction is going to take a lot more work,' added Harry.

Sandy looked out of the window. There was about an hour and a half of daylight remaining. 'It doesn't sound good for either of the New Agers at the moment.'

'So, this crazy fracas happened yesterday. Saturday, before the football started – around half past two?'

'I think so. I spoke with the cashier in the supermarket and that's what she said.'

'Do you think this Abigail woman will call you?'

'I gave her my work card with my number. She knows I'm a councillor on such matters.'

Harry nodded. 'As a counsellor, you might find that Raymond will be one of your cases when you go back to work tomorrow.'

'I've got the next two days off. Perhaps on Wednesday.'

Harry raised an enquiring eyebrow. 'This Abigail woman and the strange events have got you thinking rather intensely. These wraith things she says her husband and Mr Ballantyne were getting excited about – you don't think Abigail is partly on board with this do you?'

Sandy shook her head as she put her wine glass down. 'No, I don't think she does believe such things as fairies or wraiths. The woman is eccentric and New Age. Perhaps she thinks of herself as a bit of an Earth mother, but that's all. Something has perplexed her, and rightly so. Her husband has gone gaga, and cut his wrist in the street screaming that fairies are real.

'Raymond and Abigail had been good friends with Mr Ballantyne, and as such they would have heard such things from him regularly. Perhaps Raymond was just repeating the old, confused and twisted dogma of a troubled old man. I'm sure

Abigail wouldn't believe such things. She is a bit New Age and a Green Party supporter, she has the relevant stickers and logos on her van window, but she's no fantasist of celestial beings.'

'Then why would she have such a spell book?' asked Harry as he sipped his wine.

'Abigail bought the spell book because it was of interest to her. I think folklore in general is something she's drawn to. I doubt she believes in the myths and spells, to her they're charming and antiquated. Maybe she'd try a spell out. The one she did for Mr Ballantyne was more of an appeasing favour. In a strange way, Abigail actually helped the eccentric old man. If it was true that he believed such things, Mr Ballantyne convinced himself the spell worked – the palliative effect for a troubled mind. After all, Abigail is eccentric like Raymond. The couple are two peas in a pod.'

Harry smiled once more. He agreed with his wife and nodded. 'Raymond had never been given to shouting and making a spectacle of himself before. I've heard others talk of him. He's extremely laid-back in most people's opinion, a bit of an oddball but otherwise sound. I once heard the old barmaid, Veronica, admitting that if Raymond was any more laid-back, he'd likely topple over.'

Sandy agreed. 'I can't visualise Raymond being so strange. Not the way Abigail told me earlier, especially shouting and hollering at people. I believe her when she firmly states that it isn't in his character to behave in such a confused way.'

Harry took a deep breath as though pondering on whether he should say his next words. For a moment he lingered and then he spoke of an old memory. 'It is strange that this wraith-like fairy thing has come up again. It's not the first time such tales have been spoken of. I haven't heard such things for a long time now, not since I was a youngster. But there was a small commotion back in the past. It all died down and the dust settled on the matter.'

'You've never spoken of this before,' said Sandy, intrigued.

Harry frowned. 'To be honest, I hadn't thought on the matter since I was a kid. But you've reminded me of the incident. I must have been about seven at the time. It was also concerning a commotion in the town. I never saw it but people spoke about it. There was a vagrant called Dirty Don. He used to be a familiar sight but one day he was arrested and taken away in a police car. The man had self-harmed. He was shouting and calling for people to go to the woods. He also said there were fairies living there. He used to drink a lot and was not wired up right.'

'But you never witnessed this? You just heard others speak of it?' Sandy asked.

'This is so,' answered Harry. Then he continued, 'There was another strange old lady who wandered the forest on an old tricycle. We called her Old Maud. She had a pointed nose and used to wear a big straw hat with shaded glasses. No one knew exactly where she lived but we would often see her cycling into town most days. She would talk to us sometimes and was a kindly person. I can remember her speaking to a few friends and myself shortly after Dirty Don was taken away.'

'When you say Dirty Don, you do mean because he was unclean – or do you mean he was a little shameful in other ways?' asked Sandy.

'Oh no, he was just plain dirty and unwashed. He used to reek of body odour and everyone gave him a wide birth. However, the interesting part of this story is about Old Maud and what she said to us kids after Dirty Don's commotion – a few days later.'

Sandy's big brown eyes widened with interest but her face grimaced at the thought. Then she said, 'Go on then.'

'Old Maud told us not to disrespect Dirty Don's words, because he was saying things that she had witnessed to be true. Well, us kids thought she was just as batty as Dirty Don. But at least Old Maud didn't stink. Her clothes looked old but they were always clean. She was also rather articulate when I think back. She had an ability to hold a person's interest.'

'Did she also speak of wraith-like fairies then?'

Harry laughed. 'Old Maud did, actually. I can't remember her exact words but she insisted that Dirty Don was right about flora growing in wintertime. She said it grew quickly, in a matter of seconds. From seed to flower. On tree branches too. The old woman insisted that this was how one could tell a fairy was present in the winter. Evidently, these fairies bring joy by their mere presence. When they leave or move on, the absence causes all living things to wither and die. Old Maud told us that flowers can grow in the snow, bloom brightly in the aura of a fairy and then quickly wither and die in seconds as the supernatural creature walks off.'

'What makes people tell such tales as this?' Sandy smiled, enchanted by what Harry was telling her.

'Well, Old Maud went on to tell us that all the plants wither and die because there is something happy and vibrant within the creature's lifeforce. Something that radiates like the summer sun. It brings a joy of life. When they leave that absence of lifeforce quickly brings about death of all flora in winter. These creatures can impose this joy of life upon humans too. But they need to touch someone. Old Maud told us that Dirty Don was kissed by one such being and went mad when the little imp left him and went back to the woodlands.'

'And what happened to this Old Maud?'

Harry smiled while reminiscing about the strange old woman. 'I've no idea what became of her. I would imagine she's long gone by now. The same for Dirty Don. They were very old back then.'

'Old New Foresters remembered?' Sandy smiled.

Harry nodded and looked lost in thought. 'I should say. Good old Maud Hoskins.'

'Hoskins?' Sandy asked. 'You did say Hoskins?'

He nodded. 'Yes, Maud's surname was Hoskins.'

'And is Maud a short name for Matilda?' Sandy was frowning but there was a glint of revelation in her eyes.

'Yes, I believe she was actually named Matilda, but we all called her Maud.'

Sandy raised her hand and gently rested it on her forehead. 'Abigail's book of Witchcraft, potions and spells – she said the book was bought locally in Brockenhurst. The author was Matilda Hoskins.'

Harry smiled. 'Really! Well fancy that! It would be the type of thing Old Maud might do. She was another peculiar type, likeable but strange none the less.'

'It just goes to show how such strange myths can become folklore. Imagine in the Middle Ages. What if some peasant came running into town, back then, with such a tale?' suggested Sandy.

'I'm sure such fanciful tales were told back then. Probably ten a penny,' said Harry, laughing.

Sandy took another sip of wine and then changed the subject. 'Are you off to Holyhead for the Dublin ferry tomorrow?'

'The first meeting will be in Cork. I'll have to drive there once off of the ferry at Dublin.'

'Oh,' she replied. 'I thought you had a meeting in Dublin.'

'I do. But that's scheduled for when I return. The powers that be suggested Cork first. Then I must drive on to Dungarvan in County Waterford before travelling to the Dublin meeting. Then back on the ferry for the return. I'll be home by Wednesday evening.' He smiled.

'You'll have a fair amount of driving to do in Ireland. It will give me two days. I'll be seeing Janice again on Tuesday, but tomorrow will hopefully be a quiet day,' added Sandy.

'Things never always go to plan,' said Harry jokingly.

Sandy raised an eyebrow. 'Yes, never truer words spoken.'

CHAPTER 7

NELLY GETS HER WALK

Janice and Simon came out of the Side Wood next to their cottage to face the heathland, where the thick snowfall was settling and forming a thicker layer upon previous falls. They looked up the gentle rise towards the little cluster of trees at the top of the heath. A place they referred to as the Little Wood. They were surrounded by forest with odd patches of scattered, open heath. There were many such places, where small woods grew within the patchy heaths. They felt that these particular woods belonged to them, the Side Wood by their cottage and the Little Wood up on the heathland rise. In reality it was common land for all visitors. This was the new, wonderful place where Nelly loved to run.

Simon grinned. 'Come on then, let's go for it.'

Janice put her head down against the falling snow and called to Nelly. 'Come on, girl, follow. Up the rise to the Little Wood.'

Nelly yelped excitedly, oblivious to the snow-flakes constantly settling and melting upon her black coat.

With hoods up Simon and Janice bent into the blizzard and ascended the heath towards the small copse of trees. They continued to call and whistle through the thick snowfall for Nelly to follow. Every now and then, the happy dog would stop – there were too many interesting smells. The joyful mutt jumped amid the snow splattered ferns with a play-ful spirit that was oblivious to the cold. Occasionally, she barked with excitement, her black tail swinging from side to side. She would constantly shake her-self off from the settling snowflakes, only for the speckled whiteness to reappear in an unremitting assault of flurry-falling freshness.

'The way this is beginning to fall, we'll be pushed getting back,' said Simon laughing as Janice put her arm through his.

'This bit of heath and the path to the cottage is the only open part. I think the woods ahead will allow a little shelter, even though it's penetrating the trees.'

'We still have to get back soon,' he replied excit-edly. 'At this rate we'll be skiing.'

They pressed on up the rise where the ferns were disappearing, covered by the settling snow.

Nelly had shot off ahead of them, making for the Little Wood. New smells, new experiences. A place she had quickly become accustomed to.

As Janice and Simon followed their pet's prints towards the fringe of the Little Wood, Nelly burst out from the trees towards them. The black mutt was whining as though something had upset and unsettled her.

Simon laughed as the dog raced towards them. 'Poor Nelly, she thought she'd lost us.'

Thinking the dog was playfully excited, Janice bent down with arms outstretched to greet and make a fuss. To her and Simon's immense surprise, Nelly shot straight past them. It was as though Nelly was desperate to be away from the Little Wood and back on the heathland.

'Hey! Little Nelly girl,' Janice called. 'Come back, silly girl. What's wrong?'

Simon was as confused. 'What the hell as got into her?'

Janice stood up and looked back out onto the heath. 'Come here, you're a silly girl,' she called again.

Nelly had stopped lower down. She was looking back at them. Once again, the snowflakes began to settle across her black fur. The dog had a despairing look as though she wanted Simon and Janice to leave with her. She barked once and then began to whine, and whimper. Wanting – imploring – them through high-pitched howls of discontent not to go into the confines of the wood.

Janice laughed. 'I think something has spooked her.'

Simon was serious. 'Yes, she has been.' He looked back up, deeper into the wood and took a few paces towards the perimeter. He looked just inside the woodland where the snowfall seemed less penetrating. Within the confines of the trees, the snow was still laying, though it wasn't as heavy as on the heath. The same fresh smell of rustic wood and scented ferns was present. Simon felt the strong magical enchantment of the place as he took a few steps into the wood.

Suddenly, his heart skipped a beat. He felt the hairs of his neck bristle on his cold skin. It sent a shiver through his body. 'What was that?' he muttered to himself. Nervously, he looked around. Carefully his vision swept about the snow-covered forest floor. His attention was caught by the spectacle of a cluster of flowers at the base of a tree.

He whispered to himself, 'How could such a thing be in winter?'

Janice stopped beside him and followed his line of vision. 'Bluebell flowers in full bloom.'

'In the middle of winter with snow lying about?' Simon was perplexed.

'I know sometimes spring flowers come early, but not this early and under such conditions as snow,' Janice replied.

The bright-blue petals looked resplendent and healthy as though basking in a spring thaw. But it was heavy winter with snow falling.

Simon frowned. 'If I didn't know better, I would have supposed them to be plastic imitations. A trick that some prankster had arranged?'

Expectation and logic kicked in. Slowly Simon moved towards the floral phenomenon to investigate the conundrum further.

An intense breeze hit him from the wood. The bluster swept suddenly about and then passed as he heard the uncanny sound of infantile voices! Eerie and full of mischief. He stopped abruptly, shaking his head, dismissing the strange thing. It was a figment of his overactive imagination.

'Where are you going?' called Janice, looking about her. She'd felt the strange breeze too. Slowly they proceeded towards the cluster of bluebell flowers growing out of the snow. 'I thought I heard voices in the wind.' She looked to Simon and giggled nervously.

'Yes, I did too. Perhaps we're a little spooked.' Simon laughed dismissively. 'But I can't get over this for strange.' He was pointing to the bluebells grow-ing in the snow before them.

Janice stood beside him and looked at the phe-nomenon. She was equally astounded. 'Flowers in full bloom in the middle of winter? Snow lying everywhere, and they have grown through it? They are forest blue-bells but they can't bloom in winter – can they?'

'I don't think so, but then I don't know much about flowers. So, they are woodland flowers?'

'I think so, but then I'm sure they don't bloom in winter. I don't know much about flowers, but I'm certain this is unusual.'

'They could be plastic flowers?' Simon sug-gested. 'Our weird New Age visitors doing some ritual for the deceased Mr Ballantyne. They may have put them there when I saw them a few days ago. Perhaps they're folklore gimmicks?'

She frowned and continued to look intently at the spectacular display before saying, 'A plastic gim-mick? It would be logical.'

Slowly she moved forward as another gust of wind swept through the trees and temporarily engulfed them. Again, amid the swirling bluster, there was the distant echo of mischievous infantile laughter. It was like the distant din of a nursery, heard from the end of a long corridor.

'Did you hear that,' she whispered nervously as the gust passed on.

'It's the wind,' he replied. 'It always makes strange sounds in woodland.' He was dismissive, but Janice was not convinced by his half-hearted rationale. Simon was as unsure as she was.

'It sounded like children,' she said.

He laughed then answered, 'We're letting our imaginations run wild.'

They were still moving cautiously around the cluster of bluebell flowers at the base of a tree just inside the fringe of the wood. As they walked around the floral display, each became convinced the plants were not artificial.

Janice knelt before a flower and touched the petals. Her hand shot back and she stood up perplexed and shocked. 'It's real.'

Simon frowned, but was loathed to touch it. Instead he backed off and said, 'Let's get back to Nelly.' He licked his lips and added, 'The snow is going to fall for some time. I think it's best to get back.'

She agreed, not wanting to remain in the Little Wood. 'We've never seen these flowers before.'

'We've never come this close to the Little Wood before,' replied Simon.

'We've only done our Side Wood and the heathland below. We've only been here two weeks and the snow has been doing its thing since the day we moved in.'

Simon seemed to change his mind. 'The blue colour is very vibrant. How come we never noticed them while passing close by yesterday? I could see into the woods.'

Janice adjusted her royal blue winter beanie. 'The snow was not laying inside the woods then. Perhaps the blue didn't stand out. Maybe these bluebells have bloomed as a little cluster today? Perhaps Nelly was running about and our observation was on her? Perhaps they are winter flowers, a type of flower we don't know about? One that looks like a bluebell?'

'I hope so.' He laughed. 'That was an avalanche of explanations. But I have to admit, I'm spooked, like Nelly. But she wouldn't be afraid of flowers. They would mean nothing to her.'

'Dogs are strange,' agreed Janice. 'And Nelly's behaviour is allowing our minds to work overtime.'

Simon nodded and smiled. 'Let's get back indoors then.'

He couldn't resist another look at the flowers. Then, through some new sense of morbid curiosity, Simon stepped closer to the strange cluster. He bent down to gently touch one of the petals. His hand recoiled from the feel of the soft blue bud, as though he had done something intrusive and unnatural. The icy squall seemed to scold in protest amid the trees and the falling snowflakes. He looked up at the bleak, rustling branches and twigs, the snowflakes breaching the tree canopy to settle about the woodland. A beautiful cascading pall of white fluff. It was time to go.

'Come on,' yelled Janice through the icy bluster. She too looked up at the overhanging branches and the cascading snow. 'We'll feel better when we get back to the cottage. Even Nelly has had enough.'

Simon nodded and followed her out onto the heathland where the blizzard was in fuller force. Nelly suddenly stopped whining and began to wag her tail as they descended towards her through the snowstorm. The heathland ferns were completely buried. The thick, settling snow was overpowering everything.

They made their way back along the way they had come. The dog walk with Nelly was being cut short. The snow was too intense, more so than expected. But in truth, all three were spooked by the Little Wood.

Unseen behind them, the deserted copse of trees was still caught in the eerie howling of the winter's bluster. The strange bluebell flowers began to sway as though trying to move amid whispers of the swirling breeze. Suddenly, all the vibrant blue petals on each flower began to wrinkle and wither in a sad harmony of decay, the bright blooms fading to a deteriorating brown exhibition. Each bluebell waned and collapsed into the snow beyond the sight of the wood's recent visitors. The delicate blossom was soon gone. The foul remains of decay were gently buried by the new, settling white flurry.

Then the snow mound began to swell, and a fresh uncanny event began. More delicate flora pierced through the expanding snow where the crumpled plant husks had collapsed. A line of varied-coloured blooms. An indescribable beauty springing up. A furrow of unnatural colourful splendour – a brilliance that sprouted upon a swelling and moving mound of snow. The upsurge of eager flora bloomed in seconds, then withered and died upon the moving white course of worm-like slush. A bristling then dying tide garnished the white mound as it advanced, as though a giant mole was burrowing below. The phenomenon progressed in its slithering configuration towards the fringe of the wood amid the childlike whispers of the breeze, a supernatural entity that left a trail of tiny, dead flowers in its white wake. As quickly as the tiny petals opened, they withered and died while the head of the flourishing line moved forward. The sad, rotting peelings on the hump of the wake displayed the dead petals like corpses upon a distant battlefield.

Had the late Mr Ballantyne been present, he would have spoken the names of the numerous flowers: wood calamint, Lady Slipper, ghost orchid and crested cow-wheat with odd cornflowers. All springing up and growing in seconds and then withering to die in the next instant. Rotting in the moving mound's wake.

The moving flora followed the path of the recent and departed visitors. The sentience of the delicate floral entity halted at the fringe of the woodland as though observing the departing people.

Within the blizzard was the continuous infantile sound of distant laughter and chanting.

'*La, la, la. La, la, la.*'

CHAPTER 8

CALLING ABIGAIL'S MOBILE

At first, Sandy was a little apprehensive about calling Abigail. Perhaps the woman was still at the hospital with Raymond? Maybe a call would be too intrusive? Then she reasoned that Abigail seemed to want to speak to someone. It hadn't taken much for her to allow the traumatic story to come flooding out.

The phone rang twice before Abigail answered. 'Hello, Sandy, I'm so pleased you've called. I was about to call you,' said Abigail. She seemed excited and a little more upbeat than Sandy expected.

'It's no trouble at all, Abigail. You sound a little optimistic,' Sandy replied.

'I am, Sandy. I know this is going to sound completely potty, but I think Raymond is reacting the same way as Mr Ballantyne did after my reciting the spell and giving him the mixed herb and lemon balm concoction. I did the same to Raymond when the nurses were out of sight. It has definitely had some sort of placebo effect. Within minutes he seemed to calm and become reasonable. Even though he is sedated, the nervousness has completely gone. I don't know how to explain it. There is honestly a bizarre improvement.'

'Do you think this psychological effect will last?' asked Sandy, trying to introduce a pragmatic point of view.

'I've been thinking about that. I thought about it with Mr Ballantyne too. I keep coming back to the same conclusion – I think Raymond is beyond the strange bereaving notion of loss. Just as Mr Ballantyne overcame it with the belief in the potion and spell. Raymond also seems rational and honest like Mr Ballantyne became. They insist they were each kissed by a wraith-like fairy woman, a delicate, alluring mite that transfixes a person. Raymond no longer appears suicidal. He won't admit to what he saw to the doctors or nurses anymore. He just whispers his insistent belief to me. I don't know what else to say, but I do feel secure in the knowledge of him being in control of himself – he won't try to commit suicide anymore. But there are these wraith-like fairy creatures in the Little Wood according to him and according to Mr Ballantyne – the latter until his dying day.'

Sandy sat down in her armchair and replied, 'I know Mr Ballantyne believed in such things. He often tried to convince me in the high street when I bumped into him. He did have a matter-of-fact approach to his outrageous belief. Are you sure it's not a combination of his belief in your spell and the effects of his sedation drug?'

'I've thought on that matter too and I will return to the hospital in about forty minutes to see him again. Then I'll know a little more once I've had further opportunity to gauge his condition.'

'How will you know more, Abigail?' Sandy took a swig of black coffee. She had drunk two glasses of red wine.

'While I was there the nurse brought around Raymond's medication on a tray. She gave him some tablets and a swig of water. When the nurse walked off and continued her rounds, Raymond spat the pills into his hand. He never took them.'

'Is that wise, Abigail?' Sandy was concerned and wasn't sure why the woman remained so excited and optimistic at such behaviour.

'Raymond held my hand and reassured me that he'd be fine. He knew what he was doing and he understood the dreadful loss he'd felt when this wraith-like creature left him spellbound with a desire to protect, love and cherish. All this uncanny emotion from a quick, unexpected kiss. He said the thing had pale-blue eyes with tiny black pupils and her head moved spasmodically like a lizard or raptor. He spoke of flowers blooming in the snow around the creature as it stood before him, looking up at his eyes with hypnotic attraction. He insists it was a glimmering spell, that he was like a rabbit in the headlights. An enchantment that works on all creatures and plants. He went on to say that the spell was better than the hospital's sedation drugs. That he knew what he was doing after my spell from the book. He could make sense of things and the stupid self-indulgence of his heartfelt fixation. I know this sounds a strange thing to admit to me, his partner. But I believe he's genuine, Sandy. I believe he thinks he's right about his mental madness and why it affected him so. I think this psychological thing is working against the neurotic reaction he's had.'

'Well, I hope it is, Abigail. I'm sure Raymond is still disturbed by what triggered him in the first place, but perhaps you have done something right with this palliative approach.'

'What Raymond is saying, is that he saw a fairy. A wraith-type creature. And he's wondering if there's some gas or methane in the air, something hallucinogenic that caused his condition. He wants to find out more. Mr Ballantyne never tried to explain his strange hallucination - he chose to believe it. Raymond thinks there must be a logical explanation.'

'I see,' said Sandy. 'Perhaps something was dumped in the Little Wood. Something that is seeping a hallucinating vapour. That would make sense and it would explain why you can see Raymond's train of thought. It does seem as though reason is kicking in. However, I would still be alert. Maybe Raymond is telling you what you want to hear.'

Abigail coughed. 'I've kept this in mind too. It's what I may decipher better upon my return to the hospital. In your professional capacity, could you spot someone who was trying to hoodwink you by saying things they suppose you might like to hear?'

'I often have a good idea, Abigail. There are things I can do and there are lines of questioning I can proceed with. Why do you ask? Would you like me to visit the hospital with you?' Sandy thought it might be worth asking.

'Oh, would you, Sandy? I'd be most appreciative if you could.'

'I can do that, Abigail, and I would be glad to. I'd need you to pick me up, however, because I've drunk a couple of glasses of wine over dinner.'

'That's no problem at all, Sandy. I can pick you up wherever you like. Will you come with me?'

'Of course. I live along Rookes Lane. Do you know it?'

'I do,' Abigail replied.

Sandy gave her house number and then said her brief goodbye. She got up and went into the kitchen where Harry was packing his overnight bag for his forthcoming trip to Ireland.

'That was Abigail,' she said putting the empty coffee cup in the bowl.

'How is she?' he asked.

'A lot better than I would have expected. Raymond seems to have calmed down and is talking pragmatically about why he saw this wraith-like fairy thing. He seems to think there is something halluci-nogenic in the wood where he went. Something in the air that is powerful and strong.'

'Something to do with pollution?' he asked.

'Yes, I think that's exactly what he means,' Sandy replied.

'It seems a long way to go off of the beaten track to dump something. You did say the Little Wood is high on the heath and this Raymond fella had gone all the way up the heathland via a small walking track in the snow?'

'That's correct.' Sandy liked Harry's reasoning. He thought of obvious things that she sometimes overlooked.

'Why would this person, who dumped such a thing, walk all the way up to this Little Wood when the side wood next to your friends' cottage is on the road?'

'That is a good question,' admitted Sandy. 'He might tell an elaborate tale to get around that. I can test him with that very question. I'll know by the way he answers if he's being disingenuous. There are other questions I can put to him as well.'

'I take it you're going to the hospital then? With Abigail? You have had a couple of glasses of red wine.'

'Abigail's picking me up. I'll be gone about an hour.'

CHAPTER 9

THE RETURN TO THE COTTAGE

Down on the slope, amid the blizzard, Nelly looked up and lingered. Her tail wagged slowly. The mutt was aware of the strange and distant floral phenomenon up at the top of the rise, but was unable to convey her dismay to her human counterparts. She barked once but was called by Janice to follow. The dog was more than happy to comply as she bounded down after them and ran on past before they could reach the Side Wood by the cottage.

Simon watched Nelly in amazement. 'One minute she's breaking her neck to get out and now she can't wait to get back indoors.'

'I think it's the snow,' answered Janice. 'She's got a little more than she bargained for.'

'There was also something strange about the Little Wood. It also affected Nelly,' he added.

Janice called out against the biting wind, 'I think we were all a little spooked by the winter flowers in the snow. Because we're ignorant of the plant life in the woods, we're probably allowing our imaginations to run wild.'

Simon looked up through the leaves at the dark, grey sky. 'It'll be getting dark soon and Nelly will settle once indoors. She did act strange though.'

Janice smiled and put her arm through Simon's as they walked through the Side Wood next to their cottage. 'Perhaps, we were putting two and two together and coming up with five.'

He smiled. 'You're right. I must admit, it did feel weird when she bolted out of the wood and back onto the heathland. I suppose it was the sight of the winter flowers after all.'

They ambled back to the cottage and dismissed the strange happening as one of those odd little things that sometimes occur.

During the evening, Janice had cooked a meal, which they had both sat down to eagerly. It had been complimented by a fine red wine and both felt relaxed by the repast and began to talk of the doll's house again.

'I'm going to get some furniture and things to put inside,' Simon said. 'After all, it won't look complete without the tiny chairs, tables and all.'

'I wonder if there's a place in Lymington for such things,' added Janice.

Simon screwed his face into a doubtful look. 'I think Southampton is our best bet. It's much bigger and more likely to have what I'd be looking for.'

Janice giggled. 'You'll need a little cooker and washing machine, a three-piece and beds.' She was beginning to get excited by the charming idea. 'Southampton would be the best place I think.'

Simon pushed his chair back and stood up. 'I want to have another look at that doll's house,' he said with a smile.

Janice stood too and they both went to the cellar door, while Nelly followed, not wanting to miss out on things. The light was turned on and they descended into the cold cellar.

'We should have put coats on,' Janice said, laughing.

'Blimey, you can say that again,' agreed Simon.

They went to the work bench for a quick look at Simon's finished project. Both were already thinking of leaving due to the unexpected chill. It was much more severe than either had expected.

Suddenly, Nelly began to whine and yap as she retreated backwards towards the cellar stairs. They turned to see what was upsetting the dog this time and found Nelly's attention fixed upon the empty bottle of wine and broken glass, where Janice had left them earlier in the afternoon. To their utter surprise, both objects were covered in fine-gritted sand. It was as though glass and bottle had been smothered in adhesive then sprinkled with glittering grey dust. It completely covered all the broken shards. However, the most astounding thing was the two flowerpots sitting either side of the bottle and broken wine glass. Withered and dead geranium flowers had grown, bloomed and died in a matter of hours – while they were out walking Nelly. The deceased flower heads hung on arched stems either side of the gritted bottle and glass. They were like fallen curtains on some twisted stage – a gruesome finale to a very brief life.

For a moment they drank in the uncanny sight. Janice gulped while the silence seemed to scream at them. Each looked about the cellar expecting to see something else equally inexplicable.

'I don't believe it,' said Simon dumbfounded, moving forward to take a closer look. 'The pots were just full of dirt. Now flowers have grown and died since we took Nelly for a walk this afternoon.'

'They've bloomed and died in the winter. These are geraniums. They're not winter plants. I thought the pots were empty. The seeds must have been left in the soil – they've germinated and grown in this short space of time. Maybe it's something common to the New Forest, but I doubt it. I'll ask Sandy when I see her next. She'll be bound to know,' stuttered Janice, hoping there might be some logical explanation.

'Janice!' Simon barked, agitated by it all. 'Even if it is a winter flower, which I doubt, I don't know of anything that grows so quickly, blooms, then dies and almost rots in such a space of time.' He shook his head. 'Something's not right.'

'Stop it, Simon, please. You're beginning to frighten me,' Janice replied.

Simon gently pulled her to him and hugged her. 'I'm sure there's an explanation, Petal. I just don't know what it can be. There must be something we're overlooking. It's the flowers in the Little Wood. They've got our minds working overtime – as you have already said.'

More whining came from Nelly. She had retreated to the top of the staircase and her yelping tone was almost imploring. The mutt wanted them to come upstairs too.

Janice took a step backwards from his embrace and shook her head. She shivered from the cold and the eerie sight before them. 'Now I'm beginning to get too spooked. I can't dismiss this one. This is not natural, no matter how we try to rationalise this. Something is not right.'

This time, it was Simon who tried to be calm. 'Maybe we don't know about things in the forest…' He stopped, realising it was pointless to dismiss such a strange occurrence. 'Someone has been here,' he finally admitted.

Both became more nervous as they looked about the cellar suspiciously.

'Let's go back upstairs,' whispered Janice earnestly.

Simon nodded. 'Yes, alright and I'm locking the back door. Then I'm going to look about the house outside.'

They went back up the stairs. Nelly was sat at the top in a state of agitation, looking down the staircase into the cold cellar. The dog yelped pitifully and then did a rumbling whine again. She was unable to convey her sense of frustration. The wretched mutt could not draw their attention to the small shadow against the cellar's dirty, pale wall. There, within the pastel glow, was a shadow of a tiny female. A mysterious, crouching infantile form. A diminutive shadow that had veined wings on her back. The petite silhouette's extensions gently opened like those of a dragonfly.

Nelly followed the shafts of dismal light, the beams flowing from the cellar window. At the misty skylight pane was an angelic face – a pretty little countenance. The innocent-looking features were smooth like porcelain, a delicate and alluring visage pressed against the frosty glass. The strange blue irises had tiny black pupils, no bigger than a pinprick. The otherworldly set of eyes peered into the bleak room. A mischievous grin revealed a row of tiny white teeth and small snake-like fangs, upper and lower on each side.

Nelly's ears stood upright and her tail began to lift and drop, tapping the floor with slow, irritated perplexity. She might have started barking, but it was no use. No one took notice.

The light went off and Nelly quietly grumbled, a low growl of disapproval. The cellar door was closed and the mysterious creature at the window was blocked from view. Only Nelly the mutt had noticed it.

'Come on, Nelly, it's just an odd thing of dead flowers, broken glass and sand. It's all over now,' said Janice, ignorant of what Nelly had seen. The frightened dog scampered along the hallway.

'Dogs can sense when we're unsettled,' Simon added.

They locked the cellar door and stood back contemplating what had just happened. Were they overreacting? Had they allowed themselves to be alarmed?

Janice put her hands to her mouth and breathed through her fingers while Simon stood with his hands clasped.

'I can't believe this. What should we do?' he said.

'We can't call the police. They would laugh at us or think we were wasting their time.' Janice sighed and put her hand around the back of her neck.

Simon nodded. 'I know, but just to be on the safe side, I'm going outside to check everything. It's probably nothing and perhaps we are a couple of town dwellers who need to get used to the isolation of the New Forest.' He laughed nervously. 'Where's that torch?'

Janice laughed too. 'It's in the small table locker by the street door. I'm going to sit in the lounge and cuddle Nelly. Don't be long.'

'I'll be back in a jiffy.' He put his coat on and slipped his feet into green wellington boots, found the torch and clicked it on to make sure it worked. It was fine.

Nelly started to whine again, making it clear she didn't want Simon to go.

'Stop that now, Nelly – be a good girl and sit with me. Come on now, be a good girl,' whispered Janice.

Nelly wagged her tail compliantly and went into the living room to jump up on the sofa with Janice.

Simon went to the street door, opened it and was greeted by the cold dusk's howling wind. He turned and called back to Janice, 'I'll not be long. Stay put and don't follow.'

He went out, closing the door with a thud to make sure it was firmly shut. He even gave it a reassuring push and pull. It was firmly closed.

The last of the daylight was all but swallowed up. The winter's night was starting amid the thick snowfall.

'Crikey,' he muttered to himself. 'I'm getting way too paranoid.'

CHAPTER 10

DRIVING BACK FROM THE HOSPITAL

Abigail steered the Toyota Townace along the dark forest road, heading towards Lymington. The headlights were on full beam and the snow was falling again. Every time a vehicle on the opposite side of the road came into view, Abigail would dip her people carrier's lights until the oncoming car had passed by. Then the full beam would resume.

'Well, what are your thoughts, Sandy. You seem very concerned and puzzled. You doubt Raymond's mental recovery. Is that what it is?'

Sandy smiled and shook her head. 'On the contrary, Abigail. I firmly believe what Raymond is saying and I believe you have done something that has inadvertently helped from a psychological point of view. He seems rational and composed and is making no bones about trying to hoodwink the medical staff. I can see he's been through some trauma, but he looks like he's come to grips with himself. I also asked a few questions I thought might trick him. They didn't.'

'Do you people have a method with questions then? A way to judge someone with your professional approach?' Abigail kept her vision firmly upon the road ahead. The snow and the dark were being handled well by the old New Age lady. Sandy realised how focused Abigail was.

'We have all sorts of methods,' Sandy replied, 'for instance, I had a pre-planned question concerning Raymond's theory about hallucinogenic gas. I wanted to see how well he might try to defend the theory. If he became over-creative, I would have assumed he was trying to tell us what he believed we wanted to hear. That way I might have deduced if he was being disingenuous.

'However, your Raymond was stumped by the conundrum of dumping something up on the heath. He didn't try to vigorously find a reason to justify his line of thought. He was clearly at a loss by my suggestion of the Little Wood being a long haul to dump something. He had no excuse and didn't try to invent one.'

Abigail dipped the headlights as an oncoming car passed them by. She then put the lights back to full beam. 'You sound optimistic by his lack of reasonable excuse?'

Sandy was perplexed. 'It means your Raymond is being honest. I also can't see any type of mental failing in him. I would never have deduced he would have done something remotely suicidal a little over twenty-four hours prior.'

'Then surely it's a good thing?' Abigail seemed desperate for a positive assessment.

'It is a good thing from what I can deduce of Raymond. He'll have to stay in hospital and go through the normal mental evaluation. He is likely to be given over to someone at my practice. I'll try to make sure it's me,' said Sandy. She still had a look of concern.

'In that case…' said Abigail, while dipping her headlights again for an oncoming car. It passed and once again she went to full beam.

'In that case…?' Sandy coaxed her with a smile.

'If you think Raymond seems rational, why do I sense doubt about your evaluation?'

'Oh, I have certain doubts, Abigail. But they are not with Raymond. The things he was telling me about flora – all the plant life blooming and then withering in the snow. I have heard such things before and they're all linked. There is something strange about the Little Wood and Raymond's not the first person to have such a traumatic issue in the town centre. My husband told me of such an episode when he was a kid. It was concerning a local vagrant. My husband also spoke of a lady called Old Maud. She believed in what your Raymond saw. This old woman spoke of the same things concerning flora and being kissed by these little supernatural creatures.'

'I say, steady on, Sandy. You're not trying to tell me you believed Raymond's one failing. The one thing he wouldn't deny, even though he was insistent with a clear head?'

'I believe Raymond saw something he cannot explain. Whether it was some form of illusion that spooked him and set him off on an irrational course, I can't say. But Raymond saw something strange and diabolical. Something he can't explain. And I believe something happened to him.'

'But Raymond said he saw a wraith-like fairy – an impish little woman who quickly kissed him on the lips. An alluring supernatural being that transfixed him and sent him almost mad with sadness when the little thing giggled and ran off into the woods. A celestial being that left tiny footprints and decaying flora in her wake. Surely, you're not comfortable with that one insistence, Sandy? You can't be?'

'I'm not comfortable with the explanation, Abigail. But neither is your Raymond. Yet he will not deny it. He is telling his truth to us as he saw things. His one theory of hallucinating vapour was all he had left. I have all but taken that theory down. Raymond can't think of anything else and he is not making things up. He did see something and that book of yours has definitely helped – the spell and potion you gave him worked. I don't want to speculate how, but I have one more piece of information that might interest you.'

'I'm ready to listen to anything,' replied Abigail nervously. Once again, she dipped her headlights for an oncoming car. It passed and full beam was resumed.

Sandy waited patiently for Abigail to complete the safety manoeuvre, then she informed the anxious lady of some further information.

'Old Maud, who my husband spoke of, is Maud Hoskins. Maud being short for Matilda. Matilda Hoskins wrote that book *Witchcraft – Spells and Potions* you have on the back seat.'

'My word, the mist begins to clear,' said Abigail, clearly surprised by the new revelation.

'If I'm to be honest with you, Abigail, I believe your husband saw what he thought was a fairy. There has to be a rational explanation, but I have no idea what it is yet. For what it's worth, I want to look into this more. I want to visit the Little Wood.'

'When?' asked Abigail.

'Tomorrow. I'll visit my friend in the cottage next door to the Side Wood where you and Raymond park this vehicle. I would like you to come with me. I would also like you to bring your book. You'll meet

Janice, but we'll leave it until her husband, Simon, goes to work. He is rather conservative with his views, to say the least. Janice will prefer we visit without him being there. Of this, I'm sure.'

'Are you sure you want me to come, Sandy. I got the impression that her husband didn't want to suffer us gladly when we briefly met. Raymond and I are a couple of oddballs. We both realise that and we are aware we're not everyone's cup of tea.'

Sandy grinned. Abigail was a kindly and understanding eccentric, but in a short space of time she had developed an extraordinary fondness for the woman. She was more unassuming and interesting than she imagined.

'Well, Abigail,' Sandy began, 'I think your interests are of some importance concerning this matter. Your Wiccan interests, I mean. They are needed. I don't know why, but I have a strange feeling your book might be necessary. I would like you to come with me tomorrow and to bring your book. I'll tell Janice you're coming, so she'll be expecting you. Janice is a little more laid-back than her husband Simon. He is also a little more at ease once you get to know him. However, we'll have no male intrusion. We'll just go for a walk to the Little Wood with her dog Nelly. We'll do it at about eleven, just before midday. It will give you time for an early morning visit to see Raymond and we'll be back in time for you to see him in the afternoon. Would that be alright? I would be enormously grateful.'

Abigail smiled at Sandy and replied, 'Of course I will. I'd be happy to.'

The Toyota Townace cautiously came out of the tree clearing as the full beam headlights dipped. The streetlights of Lymington town were ahead. Sandy would be home soon.

'There is that one extraordinary chapter in Maud's book,' began Abigail. 'It ties in with a reason for Mr Ballantyne imploring me for a second home-protecting spell.'

'Really,' replied Sandy. Her interest further inflated. 'What is the nature of this home-protecting spell?'

'Well, even though Mr Ballantyne was protected from the fairy kiss, as he put it, this didn't stop the supernatural things, of his imagination, pottering about his cottage at night. He said he couldn't sleep and the little mites were becoming irritating. When he got up to confront this strange issue, the little things took off giggling and hid outside, jumping out through windows he had locked earlier and waiting outside for him to return to bed. He later insisted my second home-protecting spell worked as well. Finally, Mr Ballantyne maintained he could sleep at night. Thus, his disturbed condition was cured in two stages via two separate spells.'

Driving had become easier as they moved through the town bathed in streetlights.

Sandy raised her eyebrows. 'Yet he insisted that he still believed fairies lived in the Little Wood, despite your cure for these unseen things? He even tried to convince me on a few occasions.'

'Well, yes. Poor Mr Ballantyne continued to insist in this belief of fairies living inside the Little Wood,' replied Abigail.

'Why would they come into his cottage?' Sandy sounded amused yet also concerned.

'I have no idea, but Maud Hoskins' book suggests a sweet spot where they place a standard of sorts. Then they will come and go at night. They like to sneak around. For what reason? I can't explain. Neither does the author Maud Hoskins.'

Abigail parked the people carrier outside Sandy's home. 'Here we are, Sandy. Shall I call you after my morning visit to Raymond at the hospital?'

'Yes please, Abigail. I would be most grateful,' Sandy replied and got out of the vehicle.

'That's settled then. I'll call tomorrow. Good night, Sandy.'

'Good night, Abigail.'

Sandy watched as the battered-looking Toyota Townace pulled off and continued to Ringwood.

CHAPTER 11

THE WOODS AT NIGHT

Simon cautiously stepped off the snow-covered doorstep and wished he had stayed in the warm lounge with Janice and Nelly. He trudged out into the night through the freshly falling snow towards the Side Wood, the radiance of the house lights gently stroking the foliage of the winter woodland's perimeter. The branches swayed amid the cascading white flurry. He breathed in the cold air and felt the chilling rush in his lungs. It made him feel fresh and alert as he turned on his torch. For a brief instant, he felt fine. He had calmed down and decided he must have been overreacting. It was only for a moment, however, because then the realisation came to him.

The immature nursery noise was there, mixed with the night's winter bluster. The chanting was coming from the inner woodland – far-off infantile singing. A harmony of collective infant chanting.

'*La, la, la. La, la, la.*'

The eerie mantra was wrapped in the night's snowstorm and the rustling trees.

'*La, la, la. La, la, la.*'

Simon strained his ears and listened more intently. He was searching for something that might make him dismiss the strange, infantile chanting.

'*La, la, la. La, la, la.*'

Once again, his heart began to thump and a hollow feeling formed in the pit of his stomach. He shook his head in a vain effort to bring reason. It didn't work. The wind was still howling but the strange cacophony of high-pitched voices was still coming from the wood. The infantile singing was assuredly there. Again, like little children in a far-off nursery droning in high-pitched unison.

'*La, la, la. La, la, la.*'

Simon frowned as he strained his hearing to try and work out what might be a logical sound. Perhaps wild ponies or deer?

'*La, la, la. La, la, la.*'

He shook his head. No, this was not an explain-able noise! But then surely the wind *could* be account-able for such a strange and uncanny repetition?

'Oh, come on, God! Throw me a bone.' He gulped for he knew, deep down, it was *still* not the wind. No matter how much he tried to play the event over, he came to the strange conclusion that the diabolical chanting was unexplainable and unearthly. The winter bloom of the day was unexplainable, Nelly's behaviour was unexplainable, and the dust-covered wine bottle and broken glass were unexplainable. And now, the distant singing was unexplainable.

'*La, la, la. La, la, la.*'

He was drawn to the mysterious chanting. Even though he was afraid. How could such a thing be? Perhaps some vagrant was living in the woods and had a cassette or something. There were vagrants, but he was told they never seemed to be around in the winter months. Such wretched people were usually close to the outskirts of a town. Again, he desperately tried to make sense of it all. He tried to invent sense or something plausible. It was no use.

'*La, la, la. La, la, la.*'

He felt drawn to the puerile incantation and found himself walking slowly amid the trees, his torch sweeping the shaft of light through the engulfing darkness. He was scared and knew he shouldn't be doing this. But there was his inner will – it stubbornly took control of his legs. His lower limbs seemed to move independently of reason. This awakened a resolve that surfaced and battled, a remote doggedness that confronted his fear.

A compulsion that pressured him to overcome any reservations.

'*La, la, la. La, la, la.*'

'Christ! What is that infernal noise?' he hissed to himself.

From a hiding place within the woodland ferns, Simon was being observed. Predatory impish eyes looked through the trees. Spiteful eyes that blazed with pale-blue glee, like those of a strange nocturnal animal. The hidden being emitted an excited hiss from a small forked tongue. The loud wind easily covered the excited whisper of awe-struck wonder.

Simon's attention was focused within the bathing light of his torch. He thought something was ahead of him. He was oblivious to the strange observer's mischievous gaze, the scrutiny of wicked intent fixed upon his coat-covered back. The night and the snow hiding everything from him.

Tiny elegant fingers pulled down a clump of twigs, green leaves growing instantly and rapidly to the touch. The diminutive blue irises with pin-sized black pupils sparkled with predatory curiosity. An open mouth with soft, light purple lips whispered an excited gasp that quickly contained itself. The waif-like mouth daintily sucked in cold air with yearning excitement. The low noise was lost amid the night's bluster and the gentle, far-off infantile chanting.

'*La, la, la. La, la, la.*'

Excited and eager, the impish creature moved stealthily from cover to cover. The patter of dainty bare feet trod nimbly upon the snow, unaffected by the chill of the ice, and the little noise was drowned out by the natural wind and supernatural chanting. The wraith-like mite even giggled in whispered tones, excited and struggling to contain such wicked joy.

'*La, la, la. La, la, la.*'

The weird little being relocated from fern to tree, making use of all the cover it could find. Gradually the scamp repositioned around and to the side of Simon, quietly and stealthily stalking the prize. The man-thing was within the strange little being's mischievous aspiration. A little huntress filled with wicked desire.

'*La, la, la. La, la, la.*'

As Simon moved deeper into the dark woodland and towards the chanting sound, he began to sweat. He had the feeling he was being watched. He swept the torch beam before him – once or twice he turned and shone the torch back along the path he had walked. He just saw ferns and trees, the same sight as before him. His heart was thumping and for the first time he realised his pulse was beginning to cause greater stress. Why was he doing this? He could be back indoors with Janice and Nelly, snug upon the sofa.

'*La, la, la. La, la, la.*'

What was that compelling, yet sinister adolescent reciting? Why was it continuous, irritating, intriguing and frightening?

He gritted his teeth and stubbornly walked on. His eyes had become a little more accustomed to the dusk and trees, allowing his gaze to wander beyond the torchlight's sweep. He was absorbed briefly by this indulgence. For a few seconds he began to calm. Then a further realisation was upon him as he stood there within the darkness – his ears were familiarised too. He hadn't heeded this because there were too many other things going on, too much information to take in upon confused wits. Now his hearing was alerted to the new fact. The strange, infantile singing was not distant any longer – it was all around him. Then there was a second comprehension. He was definitely being watched. It annoyed him and he gritted his teeth and clutched his fist, trying to hold the boiling fury that began to nurture within – his own form of self-defence. He began to shake with frustration. Let it come, let it roar, he needed this. He was being observed from the darkness. The weird bastards! Who was it?

'Who's there?' he asked forcefully. 'Come out and show yourself.'

There was a brief childlike giggle. He spun sideways and made out the shrubs shaking, disturbed by someone passing. His heart skipped a beat. Some cult or commune of New Age hippies hiding within the woods? He was clutching at reason – at fringe groups of travelling weirdos. Yes, that was it. Some hippy cult! New Age eccentrics! He gritted his teeth and summoned his courage as reason began to kick in. Bloody twats and their traveller vans.

'Show yourselves!' he shouted. 'You're all a bunch of fuckwits. Come on, want to mess with me? Come on then, you bastards, try it!'

He jumped as scattered giggles came from several directions amid the darkness. He swept his torch to reveal swinging shrubs in the darkness. Someone had moved off before the beam could engulf the departed culprit in torch radiance. In the background and all about, the commotion of impish humming intensified.

'*La, la, la. La, la, la.*'

Once again, Simon gritted his teeth in anger. He was fed up with the antics and the beast within him was coming out. He hated bloody giro junkies, freeloaders who would do anything but work. Even retreat into the forest to be away from society. Blast the continuous din coming at him from the night. His anger swelled and he encouraged it. Bloody New Age hippy twats! Trendy lefty bastards, all of them.

He bellowed. 'Right, you've all had your bloody laugh. Now come out, you pathetic little shits!'

It all stopped abruptly and for a moment there was just the howling wind and the rustling bushes. Then a single little laugh.

'*Ha, ha, ha, ha, he!*'

Simon gulped. He was hoping to provoke a response. But now he had got one, he wasn't so sure. His anger faded as quickly as it had come and he began to shiver with fear as the sweat ran down his back. It was a freezing cold night with a blizzard and he was sweating with fear.

Oh God! he thought to himself. *Perhaps I shouldn't have said that.*

A gentle rumble in the ground made him stiffen and he felt the hairs on his arms and neck stand up. Then for the first time he stepped backwards. His heart was pounding and the fear had spread throughout his torso – it was like a huge bubble of indigestion trying to force its way up from his chest into his throat. Oh God! How he wished he hadn't followed the noise. He wanted to be back indoors with Janice and Nelly.

Amid the shrubs, trees and darkness ahead of him, he could see the dismal, snow-covered floor of the winter forest. He kept the torchlight fixed upon a tree and gasped at the sight of a small, snow-covered mound. It was moving. He blinked and when he looked again, the mound was closer, like a white molehill slowly coming towards him. Tiny, exquisite, purple and pink flowers grew out of the snow. In seconds they bloomed, withered and died at the head of the moving mound, minute dead flowers fading in the snow mound's wake. It was wickedly beautiful and transfixing.

Simon was in awe of the beauty, while deep inside his reason implored he should run. His fixation held firm as he stood waiting. The floral-popping snow mound continued, moving slowly and elegantly towards him as his torchlight lent the phenomenon a bizarre stage-struck spotlight. The bubble of fear swelling in his chest grew as the mound of inter-changing floral colour drew closer. Within the sight of the dreaded singularity, he was paralysed. The unearthly wonder rumbled towards him. The rolling manifestation had a vivacity that he felt sure contained something of further supernatural dread. He wanted to turn away but still, he could not. It was something he must fear, yet still he was compelled to know what diabolical entity might be contained within the mound of snow covered with tiny, budding flowers. He felt like a fly caught in a web and he remained powerless as the snow wave of surfing and dying flowers came to his feet and stopped. A brief pause, for a split second. Then an explosion of ice crystals and flower petals erupted about him, cascading down and around his spellbound person.

His high-pitched scream was lost in the winter blizzard, engulfed and muffled by trees and the swirling snow – lost in the dark woodland. No one heard the feeble cry in that little hidden abode.

Indoors, Janice and Nelly were huddled up in front of the television watching a quiz show. Simon would be back soon and both had calmed with the white noise of the television.

As the key went into the front door both Janice and Nelly looked up happily – they had calmed down some time ago and Simon's return was the complete end to it all. For a moment.

Simon came into the living room looking extremely traumatised, wet and dishevelled. He looked as though he had fallen over and been rolling about in the snow. He was blabbering incoherently and crying like a love-sick little boy filled with an inexplicable look and sense of intense sorrow.

'My God, they are such wicked little things. Please don't go out there, Janice. You must not go outside.' He broke down sobbing and slid down the wall into a pitiful crouching heap.

CHAPTER 12

ABIGAIL'S KITCHEN

Abigail had managed to gather some of the dried lemon balm that she had stored during the summer. She used it for her tea consumption mostly but kept other herbs too. Now, her selection of lemon balm was being used for a different reason. Her cooking pot was simmering away on the gas cooker and she was tipping quantities of crushed lemon balm into the bubbling water and adding malt vinegar. A smaller selection of crushed herbs was waiting for addition in little piles – all ingredients of her new spell, one she was following from a book under the kitchen's bright strip light. Outside, it was night and snowing.

She sighed to herself. 'I can't believe I'm actually doing this. I'm the complete witch from a children's story.'

Turning her attention away from the book, Abigail observed herself in the reflection of the kitchen window. Was she going mad? No! She was perfectly sane. Something strange had happened to Raymond and her spell had worked. She kept trying to dismiss the whole thing and use the trusted placebo reason. It didn't work. Not this time. She could dismiss it with the late Mr Ballantyne some years back, but this time it was different and much more personal. Raymond was a lovable rogue with genuine qualities. He was rough around the edges character-wise with an honesty that was direct and brutal. He indulged all her Wiccan interests but didn't necessarily believe in them. In fact, he would often ridicule them. For Raymond to want her to put a spell on him was very strange indeed. For Raymond to become neurotic and suicidal was even stranger. Now his intense melancholy was gone after her potion and spell recital. Yet Raymond remained adamant that a small wraithlike fairy creature had given him a hypnotic kiss. A forever-smitten kiss. Something unavoidable and compelling of devoted affection, installing some never-ending hurt. He kept insisting there was something binding about the strange creature's quick kiss. It was wicked and charming. Beautiful and diabolical. This was where Abigail was struggling with her pragmatic sense. She believed Raymond was cured of the spell, yet he remained adamant about the supernatural being. Level-headed and dismissive Raymond insisted that fairies were real – her man of brutal honesty. Yet he was convinced that fairies were material. Maybe there was another explanation. Perhaps she should indulge the theory and follow the book. If it was all over nothing, then nothing would be lost except the time she was spending preparing an anti-fairy potion from her book.

The herbal grinder was on the table before her with various other tools. But most unusual were four plastic washing-up bottles. She had removed the four screw-on squirting tops and laid them neatly to her side.

Her mobile phone rang and a twinge of delight filled her with hope. It was Raymond's name on the display screen. He was still alright. His reaction to the spell and potion was very uplifting. Would it still be so? Had he remained in the hospital, as sternly instructed by her?

'Hello, Raymond, are you OK?'

'I'm fine, Abigail. I keep telling you. Whatever it is you put in that stuff, it works. There are no signs that it's wearing off either. There is something in that brew, Abigail. You've actually done a spell that I know works. I've sneaked of into the toilet cubicle for privacy.'

'The truth of the matter is, I'm not sure what has happened, Raymond. You were extremely unhinged. Unhinged is the best way I can put it, but you and I know that this was very out of character for you. Yet still, now you're no longer suicidal or melancholy, you maintain that you saw a wraith-like supernatural female creature. A fairy of about three and a half feet tall. I know you're not filled with sorrow anymore. I can see you're almost back to yourself.'

Raymond sighed resignedly. 'Abigail, I would never try to convince or lie to you, but I saw a strange impish little thing. It was like a girl that is no longer a girl, but not quite a woman. A giggly, smiling thing. It had a crude tight-fitting frock made of cobwebs. Thick, wavy strawberry-blond hair—'

'Cobwebs?' Abigail cut in.

'Yes! As though an army of spiders had woven her this greying white frock that was uneven and shredded about the top of her legs and also frayed about her neck. A threadbare look with shredded sleeves that stopped about at her elbows. Behind her were these exquisite transparent wings that flickered like a dragonfly. Her look was compelling and wicked. I know this sounds utterly ridiculous but Mr Ballantyne was telling the truth. He lied about nothing and his insistence on your spell working was correct. I can't believe I'm saying this to you, but I'm not making up stories, Abigail. I wish I was.'

'I always thought I'd be pleased to hear you say such a thing about one of my spells, but now, I'm not. I think there is a placebo effect concerning the spell. The main ingredient of lemon balm expels melancholy with a vapour spread inside the blood. It washes through the heart and into various arteries…'

'Stop trying to sidestep the issue with science, Abigail,' scolded Raymond. 'That is pragmatic. That is what I do. Now, pragmatic has been blown out of the water. You have finally hit on something with your spells and potions and now you're trying to dismiss everything. You got this Wiccan thing right, Abigail. Please try to understand this – you have done a spell that works.'

Abigail took a deep breath. 'I've been making various concoctions and I also need to do a spell on that house again. The book says that if the owner leaves his or her spell-protected property then the said property becomes vacant to the spritely creatures once more. That is until a new spell is recast for the new occupants.'

'I can't imagine you knocking on the door, Abigail, and asking permission from the new owners to do such a thing. I'm fairly certain what that dog walking fella is likely to say to you.'

'No, neither can I expect them to welcome me with open arms, especially using Wiccan Witchcraft as an excuse. However, I will make the necessary concoctions in case something occurs when I visit the cottage with Sandy tomorrow. After I've seen you in the morning, of course.'

'Do you think that mental health lady is trying to analyse us? She might think we're nothing more than a textbook study from her professional perspective.'

'To be honest, Raymond, maybe Sandy does. However, there is a serious aspect to her interest and concern. I believe she's beginning to think there is something strange going on.'

'Well, her thinking us a couple of oddballs is her notion of something strange going on. But at least she seems to be on board. I suppose it doesn't matter what perspective the lady is coming from if she's opening doors for us. Your major problem is trying to convince that new couple to do a spell on the house. Perhaps you can do one without them knowing.'

'I've thought of all these things, Raymond, and I could do the spell in a locked bathroom within six to seven minutes. I'll have privacy for such a small ritual in a confined place.'

'Thank God for the good old trusted ablutions,' added Raymond with a note of humour.

'Well, hearing you refer to the place as ablutions is rather polite and refreshing for you, Raymond.'

'Oh, you'd prefer me to call it the shi—'

'Shut up! There is no need to spoil it.'

'I knew you were going to say that.' He laughed.

'I've got some empty plastic washing-up squirter bottles too. Four of them. The book says that a small squirt of the lemon balm potion makes little fairy folk recoil in disgust. Evidently, such wraith-like creatures have an abhorrence to it. That's the part of me that is struggling with your side of the story. I honestly don't expect to meet these things and still cling to the hope that there is some other reason for what happened to you.'

'I wish I could get out and go with you,' added Raymond. 'What are the washing-up bottles for then? Don't tell me you're going to use them as close-quarter fairy-fighting water pistols?'

'Yes, real fairy liquid made with real lemon balm and other things.'

'Blooming hell, Abigail. What are you equipping yourself with? A do-it-yourself Rambo fairy-fighting kit? Gordon Bennett! I've heard it all now,' he said, laughing.

'I'm heartily pleased to see your melancholy mood is completely gone and your good old cynical self is alive and kicking! I don't expect to use this and I sincerely hope there's a logical and pragmatic solution to it all.'

'Like what?' Raymond asked again.

'I don't know,' she admitted. 'I rely on you for all the brutal honesty, but on this one occasion you seem to be the fantasist and I'm trying to be pragmatic. It's a complete role reversal and I'm struggling with the notion of indulging you along the lines of supernatural belief.'

'I know, but if you are going back to that place and the Little Wood, you'll hear that infantile chanting again. You'll see them, Abigail. As sure as God made little green apples. You will see them and then you'll know.'

'I sometimes curse the day that Mr Ballantyne ever came to us with his unusual request.' She sighed.

'No, you don't, Abigail. Your spell worked and you gave the old man great peace of mind. It's the kiss that one must avoid and you neutralised it. You did a lot of good things for Mr Ballantyne. You need to do it again for the new couple too.'

Abigail nodded, even though Raymond couldn't see her. 'There is one other worry. If I don't get the house spell done, the little things of the Little Wood can achieve a dominance over the property, one that would drive the new couple from their cherished home. I think it was what Mr Ballantyne feared the fairy folk might try after we destroyed his fairy-kiss enchantment.'

'Have you read all of this in that book?' asked Raymond.

'Yes, each spell is for a different purpose. One for destroying the effects of a fairy kiss. Another to disperse fairies closing in on you. It creates a safe area for a limited amount of time.'

'What on earth is this dispersal spell? You never said about that one before,' Raymond grumbled.

'I need a dead carrion bird for such a spell. A raven, or crow, or rook. But the third spell. The one I need to do, is for permanent home protection. It means the creatures can't trespass on one's property. A respect for property boundaries is evoked for the owner's entire stay within the said home. This is a crucial spell for ongoing future respect.'

'Will these little imps try to prevent that then?' asked Raymond.

'According to the book they will. They'll try to invade the home and stop it. But they didn't do such a thing when Mr Ballantyne's home spell was done.'

'It was in spring. There was no snow and Mr Ballantyne said they were more frequent in snow. You did the spell to neutralise the kiss in winter when it was snowing. He then complained that they kept coming to the house at night and were chanting and giggling. That is when he persuaded us to reluctantly go back. Remember, you were indulging him again. Or so we both believed. You did both spells a couple of weeks apart. The end of the snow and the beginning of spring.'

'It says in the book that the fairy folk are more numerous in snow too. Mr Ballantyne certainly observed that point. If fairies are real.' Abigail was still trying to be pragmatic, but somehow, the Wiccan aspect of her beliefs also battled her reason. And there was the unusual circumstance of Raymond's support too.

'Everything is going arse about face for you, Abigail,' said Raymond, reading her sudden silence.

'It always comes back to arses with you, doesn't it, Raymond. I hope one day, you'll want to do something right and find one of your arse wisecracks a major stumbling block.'

'Don't include that in one of your spells. I'd prefer you to leave my ar—'

'Enough!' called Abigail as she heard door knocking from the phone.

'I'll have to go, Abigail. That's a nurse knocking on the door and I'm still on their suicide watch list. I think they're panicking because I've been in here too long.'

'I'll see you tomorrow, Raymond. Take care of yourself.'

'Will do, love you loads.' He clicked off.

Abigail got back to reading her book and completing her peculiar preparations.

CHAPTER 13

THE EARLY MORNING PHONE CALL

S andy was relieved when Abigail answered the phone. It was early, just turning quarter past seven in the morning. It was still dark as she drove her Range Rover along the forest road towards her friend Janice's house.

'Abigail, it's Sandy. I'm dreadfully sorry to call you at such an early hour, but I have an emergency with my friend Janice and there's a change of plan concerning today's time. My husband had just driven off when I got a phone call from Janice – that was half an hour ago.'

'Oh, that's fine about time, Sandy. I'm always up early anyway,' Abigail replied.

'It's Janice's husband, Simon. The exact same thing happened to him. Like your Raymond, Simon cut his wrist last night. Janice phoned the emergency services while trying to restrain her husband. Evidently there's blood all over the kitchen and it's been touch and go through the night to save Simon. He lost a lot of blood, but the emergency services got there in the nick of time.'

'Oh my God!' Abigail was completely shocked. 'Are you going there right now?'

'I'm driving there now. I have you on loudspeaker, Abigail. But I desperately want you to come too. I doubt we'll see much of Janice because she's been up all night at the hospital. But I would like to visit the Little Wood with you, and I still want you to bring that book and be ready to do the spell. There is something ultra-weird going on. I'm assuming Janice might need to sleep after the night she's had.'

'Yes, Sandy, I'm certain your friend will need to sleep. Whether or not she can, is another matter. I have everything ready still – I did it all last night. I can come over straight away if you wish me to.'

'That would be good of you, Abigail. I think you'll be right about sleep. I'm sure Janice is going to want to take Nelly for a walk first. If I can get there quick enough, I'll offer to take the dog for a walk while hopefully persuading her to sleep for a while.'

'Alright,' said Abigail. 'I'll be as quick as I can. What shall I do, knock on your friend's front door? Suppose she's gone to sleep?'

'I'll send you a text. If she decides to sleep, I'll take the dog on my own to the heathland and text you this. If Janice decides to come with me, I'll text that. Either option, I'll let you know.'

'Alright, Sandy. That sounds like a good way to go about things. I'll be on my way.'

'You're a star, Abigail,' said Sandy, then she pressed the Bluetooth connection off on the steering wheel.

With a sense of urgency, she drove along the forest road towards her friend's house, the sludge of the settled flurry sloshing beneath the tread of the vehicle's wheels. Soon the familiar scenes of recognised landmarks reassured her. She was getting closer to Janice's cottage. Hopefully, Janice would still be up. Sandy had informed her she was on her way, but understandably Janice was confused, tired and very anxious.

Minutes later, Sandy had managed to drive her car up the slippery drive where the snow had been crushed to ice due to the recent activity of vehicles that had been up to her friend's cottage. One of the vehicles, no doubt, was the ambulance that would have rushed Simon to hospital. What a morning this would be. Poor Janice! What on earth had got into Simon?

To Sandy's relief, Janice came out of the door. She looked drained while brushing her close-fitting jeans with her brown sheepskin gloves. Then she proceeded to push her foot into one of the brown boots, which she was impatiently trying to put on. She was flustered and seemed in a hurry to be out. Even her light-blue puffer jacket was not yet zipped against the cold, late-January weather.

Her black Labrador bitch, Nelly, was wagging her tail and jumping about excitedly beside her. Nelly was pleased to be out, at last. The dog seemed oblivious to the serious events that had occurred earlier during the night. Janice smiled with relief at the sight of Sandy's white Range Rover and walked towards the car, almost slipping in her endeavour to get to the vehicle.

'Oh, Sandy, thank you for coming and I'm sorry to call you out on such a day. There's more snow to come according to the weather forecast.'

Sandy got out of the car, full of concern for her good and much valued friend. 'Don't be silly, Janice. I was desperate to come here when I heard the dreadful news. How is Simon? You said he will pull through.'

'Oh, he'll be fine physically but his state of mind is still very bad. They had to stop the blood loss then replenish and give him more blood. For many hours it was touch and go,' replied Janice. 'I just don't know what has come over him. I can't get my head round the fact that Simon tried to commit suicide. Of all people, him? Never! But he has. I keep expecting to wake up and find this is all a dreadful dream.' She looked down at her dog. 'I have to take Nelly out. She's been locked in alone all night and into the morning. Do you mind if we walk for a while? I can tell you what's been happening during the night. This is exceptionally creepy, especially with all this talk we had concerning Mr Ballantyne.'

'Of course, I don't mind a walk, Janice. It'll be nice to get some fresh air,' replied Sandy, opening the back door of the car to reach for her fawn-coloured duffle coat and wellington boots she always kept in the boot. 'This brisk cold air will be refreshing for us both. I just need to make a quick text. I have a friend coming here. I need you to meet this person.'

Quickly Sandy texted Abigail of her intended walk with Janice. She then proceeded to put on her coat, pulling out her cascading pixie locks to let them fall freely over the beige hood. Then quickly and with well-practised ease, Sandy changed her trainers for the wellington boots.

'There!' she said and stood beside Janice and Nelly waiting to go along the small, narrow pathway that led towards the side woodland – the perimeter of which began a few yards from the cottage. Nelly was jumping about excitedly and running off along the woodland path.

'Who's your friend that's coming over?' asked Janice.

'Abigail, the New Age lady. Her husband Raymond had the same thing happen to him. The same thing that happened to your Simon. Raymond cut his wrist after a strange episode in the Little Wood, the day you saw her in the people carrier with the engine running.'

'Did he speak of strange little fairy folk. The very things you told me of concerning the late Mr Ballantyne?'

'Yes,' replied Sandy. 'And he is still insistent about the matter. He's recovering in the very hospital where Simon is. I went to see him with Abigail last night.'

'I don't know what to think or say, Sandy. But something incredibly strange is going on. Let's go through the Side Wood for the heathland.

'Nelly doesn't seem upset by what has happened during the night,' Sandy said.

'Oh, she was at first. But she seems to have calmed down. Back to her normal scatty self.'

Janice and Sandy followed Nelly into the woods and continued to talk.

Janice began to tell her story. 'Simon started acting very strange last night. But even stranger and more bizarre things occurred to us yesterday. This was during the day, but then everything went totally crazy during the night. The snowfall, as you know, has been heavy over the days. At first it was wonderful. Now, it's as though our spirits have withered and died within this snowy weather. All in a mad, crazy day and night.

'Yesterday, during the night and after some bizarre antics, he did his crazy things and tried to cut his wrist. It goes back to earlier in the day when we were caught out in the snowstorm with Nelly. We went up on the heath, towards the Little Wood. We had a few strange experiences and quickly returned. At home, after dinner, we came across further strange things that spooked us. We got a little paranoid over something silly, and the upshot of it all caused Simon to go out and reconnoitre around the cottage. The night had set in about an hour beforehand. It was during the night that Simon finally lost it – everything from the day finally culminated at this time. That was when all this trauma *really* began. The snow grew more intense and a few odd things had caused this consequence. It was all the howling of the wind and the snowfall, the isolation and all. We had both got a little spooked – I was uneasy most of all.

'Well, Simon went to check the outside of the cottage. He was trying to reassure me. We both thought someone had been trespassing in our house and on our land. Simon went out into these woods during the night when it was snowing again. He was gone for about twenty minutes. When he came back, he was so traumatised and agitated. I've never seen anything like it. He couldn't talk any sense. No matter what approach I tried, I couldn't get any logic from him. He kept babbling about going into the woods and then breaking down and crying before he could finish. There was nothing coherent. He tried on countless occasions, but he couldn't form any proper explanation. He kept crying like a baby. It was a dreadful and ghastly sight. It wasn't Simon at all. I've never seen him cry. I've never seen any grown man or woman weep with such sorrow.'

'Why was he gone for so long a time? Why did he not try to get back? It's not that far from here,' asked Sandy.

'I don't know – I think it was his intention to look about for a short while, assess if anyone was about and then get back. But something caused him to linger. Trust me, Sandy, something strange caught his attention. The snowfall was very heavy, but not so bad that he couldn't make it back to the cottage. After all, he was only here in this very wood. It's very close to the house as you can see.'

Sandy looked about and up through the leafless tree branches into the overcast sky. 'Well, I would suppose at night and during a snowstorm, in howling winds, everything becomes different. Poor

Simon, I don't think I'd fancy coming into the wood in such conditions.'

Janice nodded in agreement as they walked on. 'I thought he was going to walk around the house and garden. I don't know why, but for some reason, he was compelled to check this area in this wood. Nelly and I cuddled up on the sofa and watched television. We were calming ourselves down and feeling better because Simon was checking and would be back soon. He kept muttering between his sobbing. He was babbling about childlike singing when he staggered back. I managed to get snippets from him.'

Sandy frowned. 'What did he mean by that?'

'I don't know, Simon just kept mumbling. He looked awful, as though he had fallen over in the snow. He was completely traumatised, as I said. I tried to calm him down but he kept trying to alert me to the fact that we mustn't go back on the heath where the Little Wood is.'

'Why?' asked Sandy, looking perplexed. 'What did he see?'

Janice shook her head. 'I don't honestly know. At first, he was mumbling incoherently about how he thought it was New Age travellers. You know how right wing he can be. I thought he was saying that a weirdo cult of travellers was camped close by, but then he changed. He started to say other things.'

'What things?' Sandy asked.

'Well, he then said it was not New Age travellers, but I can't say more. He wasn't himself, but I was more inclined to believe the New Age traveller story might be along the right path. You know, a passing cult community of strange veggie-eating wanderers. I was more intent on persuading him to go to bed. I was worried for him.'

Sandy nodded and put a reassuring hand on Janice's arm. 'How do you think the New Age travellers brought about his circumstance? Are you trying to say these people caused some sort of trauma that made him cut his wrist?'

'It was the only thing I could string together to make sense. Though Simon never said so in such words. He was mumbling about how he thought it might have been such people, but he was out of his mind and he looked as if he'd fallen over and suffered a blow to the head, though I couldn't find any bump or injury. And then he said he was mistaken and he shouldn't have provoked these wretched things.'

'Wretched things?' Sandy looked more astounded and she knew that Janice was holding some of the information back. She decided not to push her too much. Let her talk. It'll all come out soon.

Janice continued. 'I knew something strangely disturbing was wrong with him. I tried to get him to take me through these woods and out onto the heath, but he refused to go. Even when I tried to drag him out, he became enraged. He kept shouting about the flowers, in his own words: "Those fucking flowers are for real."'

Sandy frowned but said nothing. She knew Janice was going to tell all but was trying to find a way of putting it.

'We saw bluebell flowers in full bloom in the Little Wood,' added Janice. 'It was during the day and before the crazy night. Spring flowers in full bloom and in the middle of winter. This flora had grown through the snow. This spooked us along with the howling wind and fresh snow that had started. Nelly was whining and unsettled too, which added to it all. But later, and especially after the nighttime antics, I began to grow more concerned about Simon, more so as the night went on. He started getting neurotic. I had managed to get him to bed after considerable encouragement and got him to take some ibuprofen. He kept muttering in his sleep and was twisting and turning.'

'Did he say anything that you can remember?' asked Sandy.

Janice nodded and frowned with confusion. 'He kept whispering that someone – a girl, he later said, was very wicked and not to let them kiss you.'

'When did he say it was a girl?' Sandy seemed equally confused.

'He kept talking in his sleep. It was the first time he seemed to speak without breaking down and sobbing. I tried to ask more and press him on the matter,' replied Janice. 'He wasn't trying to deny anything, but he was acting like a little boy, even in his sleep, and I know he couldn't have been having some secret meeting in a blizzard. He was still confused, like he was suffering from the effects of an illegal substance.'

'Is that what you think?' Sandy accepted something was not right. Simon had been acting completely out of character. Janice was right. A secret meeting with another woman did seem far-fetched. 'He must have been incoherent still. Do those magic mushrooms grow in these woods?'

'I don't know, Sandy, but I doubt Simon would know of them or even how to find them in a snowstorm. In the end, I wanted to go to this wood on my own to see what might have caused such fear, but again Simon was so spooked. Even though he was semi-asleep, the mention of my intention roused him. He began to panic and physically tried to restrain me from doing this. As I got out of bed, he got up too. I just wanted to get to the bottom of what was making him so messed up. I had to scream at him to leave me alone. We almost came to blows. He was so pathetically desperate to stop me going outside, even to these woods next to our cottage.

As I left, Nelly began to bark at me from inside the house as though she was trying to persuade me not to go. I know that all sounds mad but she seemed very excitable too, and she wouldn't budge from the house, like Simon.'

'So, you went out to see if you could find out what upset Simon,' added Sandy, listening intently as a deep frown etched across her forehead.

'Well, I thought he might have seen more winter flowers or a New Age campsite or something. I was so worried,' she continued as they passed through the snow-covered trees and the forest ferns that lent a fresh rustic smell due to the dampness of the cold air. 'I did find a line of dead flowers back upon the heath. Close to this wood. Frozen pink and purple petals from the type of flowers we see in summer. Not like the ones we saw in the Little Wood. This was strange but I don't think these things could have made him so mentally unstable. When I got back, he was anxious and imploring of me not to do such a thing again. I sat him down and tried to ask him what happened, and he just muttered, "I don't know."

'I pressed him further on the matter and asked why he spoke of a strange girl and New Age followers. He became agitated and began scolding me, saying that he only thought it was New Age travellers but the little impish girl was real and to leave him alone and to let him think it through, back home.'

'Back home?' Sandy seemed bemused.

'Back home, to London.'

'I presume you pressed him further.'

They trudged out of the wood onto the open heathland and stopped for a moment to look up the soft white-layered scarp where a small cluster of trees stood.

'That's the Little Wood where we saw the strange flower in full bloom in the winter snow.'

'Oh, I see,' replied Sandy, seeming a little unimpressed by the tree cluster on the heathland's summit. 'I know of it, as you know, but have never been there. So, did you press him further about wanting to go back to London?'

'Of course I did, and I continued to press him as I tried to get him back to bed. I was trying to make sense out of the confused, unbelievable things he was saying. He continued to be vague. I knew he was holding back. I would ask a question two or three times before he would answer. It was like I didn't exist or he was pretending I was absent. I had to impose myself upon him to get him to talk and even then, he'd get cross and babble about weird and strange things from the Little Wood that had ventured down to this wood by our cottage. I became angry and thought he was being pathetic and self-indulgent. I started to lose patience with the stupid things he was saying and the melancholy mood was oppressive. It's hard to describe. He kept whispering things to himself – creepy things.'

'Such as?' asked Sandy.

'He kept muttering, "That's why flowers wither and die," and, "Such a wicked and naughty little thing." This intense paranoia just happened after returning traumatised from this very wood we have walked through. Not the Little Wood we are approaching now. His actual fear appears to be of the Little Wood, or so it seems. He thinks all the strange things originate there and come down the heath to this side wood next to our cottage.' She sighed and hesitated as though uncertain if she should continue.

'Go on, Janice,' coaxed Sandy. 'I'm listening.' They began to trudge up the heathland towards the cluster of trees at the summit.

'He said, "Everything her light radiance touches brings life. And when her glow passes by, those living things wither and die with the sadness of it all." I tried again. This time I was able to calm him down and coax him gently upon the matter. I had to speak to him like he was a little boy and I his mother or teacher. I enticed him to tell as though he was an infant. I couldn't get any straight answer from him. He just kept babbling, "That's why flowers wither and die when touched by her light."'

Sandy shook her head in disbelief. 'Simon is a very brash person. Cocky and full of life. I can't even begin to visualise him being melancholy or introvert in any way. Who was he speaking of?'

'I'm not sure what or who he was referring to. I have never seen him so dispirited but I swear it is true. Honestly, the things that came out bit by bit. He would also mutter, "Stars are dull in night-time skies." He thought I couldn't hear him. As I said, he was fidgeting and very restless. He seemed drunk and kept mumbling to himself. When I got him to bed again, his sleep was still troubled. He was tossing and turning all night. I was never going to get any sleep listening to him.

'Eventually, it came to a head again and we had another frightful argument. He came out with the most ludicrous story. It reminded me of what we spoke about concerning Mr Ballantyne, yesterday morning, when you came to see me.

'Simon started imploring me to believe that as he went into the wood, at night during the snowfall, he began to hear infantile laughter, like the sound of children in a nursery in an unseen room along a distant corridor. Those were his exact words.'

Again, Sandy frowned as they continued to trudge up the heath through the deep snow. 'Go on,' she said, her interest totally captured.

'He said he was compelled to go into the woods outside our cottage where he could hear the sound of infantile and high-spirited laughter. He said he was afraid and yet drawn to it, still knowing that something uncanny was approaching. Then he started babbling about a small aurora amid the snow-covered ferns. As this illuminated mound of snow moved, summer flowers rose up through the ice, the way they do in nature documentaries when they film a flower blooming on speeded-up time frames.'

'What did you say when he began to talk such nonsense.' Sandy was astounded that Simon, of all people, could say such things. He had to be having some sort of mental breakdown.

'I listened to him because I'd hardly been able to get him to talk clearly since his return and suddenly, he was coming out with this drivel. I wanted him to keep talking the nonsense until he had burned himself out. Then I hoped I might be able to reason with him.

'He went on, saying that the radiance began to move towards him and the infantile voices grew louder and more excited. And, as the light came closer, so more flowers rose up out of the snow as the brightness swept above. In the wake of the light, the flora that had grown and blossomed by the spectre's touch then withered and died with the light's passing.

'These are Simon's exact words to the best of my memory. He then said the ball of light stopped before him and sank into the snow as a mound of flora and green shoots arose before his very eyes. He kept muttering, "Such wonderful colours," between sentences and that the flowers swayed like they were alive and dancing to the delight of the childlike laughter that was echoing all about him.

'Then the snow erupted like steam and he was showered in cascading petals. Again, he kept muttering: "Such wonderful colours."

'Then he started to get hysterical, talking gibberish and stuttering about a small impish-looking female of about three feet tall crouched before him on a slender tree branch within the falling debris. A delicate, fragile-looking thing with angelic looks and long, unkempt golden hair. He said the impish thing had tiny pointed ears protruding either side through her hair. This infantile thing had a small, slight girl's body but her head looked like that of a woman. A young woman with an underdeveloped body that was covered in a frock made of layers of frosted cobwebs. Again, he drifted, muttering about the little sparkles upon the frock. He said, "Not quite a woman and no longer a child."'

'You sat there and listened to this?' Sandy felt herself becoming annoyed with Simon for saying such things, but also concerned that his mental state must be more severe and he might attempt suicide again if he was not closely watched and supported.

'You won't be able to cope with this by yourself, Janice. You're going to need help with Simon.'

Janice nodded and looked up as the Little Wood came closer with every laboured step through the snow. 'He even said that her head turned sideways spasmodically as she scrutinised him with movements like that of an owl or a lizard – "Quick, slight movements," he kept muttering. She also had big light-blue eyes with tiny pin-sized black pupils. She had an impish smile with tiny fangs, and soft white skin. He prattled on about being transfixed in her hypnotic stare and that as she contorted her shoulders, transparent wings opened behind her back, like those of a dragonfly. It was a brief thing, he said and then they folded down behind her out of sight. Then, in one fleeting and graceful movement, her neck lurched forward placing her face before his and she quickly kissed him before jumping backwards and disappearing into a bright ball of light from which came more of this disobedient laughter. Then he muttered, "You must never let them kiss you. You will fall in love forever and her absence will destroy you."'

Sandy shook her head in disbelief. 'He has never taken drugs or smoked any weed, has he? Some of that stuff can make people think and say stupid things. Even Mr Ballantyne never said things like that.'

Janice shook her head. 'Simon wouldn't take an aspirin. You know the way he is about any type of stimulant. He doesn't even like drinking. That's why I think the New Age traveller angle might have something. Simon can be very politically incorrect and if he started shooting his mouth off, maybe they might have overpowered him. Forced something on him to make him trip out.'

'That sounds even more far-fetched, Janice,' added Sandy. 'There has to be a logical explanation and it must stem from his going into the woods.'

'Well, must I believe the other explanation he told me? I also saw strange flowers in the winter snow. Flowers in full bloom.' Janice looked to her friend.

Sandy scratched her head and laughed. 'Well I'm sure I don't believe this story he's telling about being kissed by, what sounds like, a fairy and having his soul smitten forever. It's as though he's indulging himself in the fantasy of a child's fairy tale.'

Janice, who had never been one for children's stories, frowned. 'Is that what fairies do then?'

Sandy smiled. 'Yes, according to some fables. If a mortal is kissed by these supernatural creatures, he or she is hopelessly smitten forever.'

'Simon reads a lot and is always going on about certain thrillers and things, but he doesn't read children's fiction.'

Again, Sandy laughed. 'Whether he does or doesn't is irrelevant, Janice. I'm just quoting folklore.'

Suddenly Nelly yelped from behind. Both turned to see that the dog was sitting in the snow some way behind. She had just stopped and it was apparent she didn't want to go further.

'Come on, Nelly,' called Janice. 'Don't start all this again.'

Sandy lent her voice to the persuading. 'Come on, Nelly.'

It was no use. The dog just yelped as though wanting Janice and Sandy to come to her.

'Oh, let's just go on,' hissed Janice crossly. 'If she doesn't come, she'll go back to the cottage.'

'So, the dog doesn't like the Little Wood either.' Sandy laughed indulgently.

'To be fair, Nelly and I were spooked by this place and the cellar back home, especially with the winter flowers,' Janice said. 'But that all seems rather irrelevant after these events.'

'I must say, you are baffling me with these winter flowers,' said Sandy.

Janice related what she'd seen in the Little Wood and the strange sight of the withered flowers in the plant pots in the cellar.

Sandy frowned and admitted such things seemed odd. Very odd indeed as they turned and continued towards the bleak woodland with Nelly barking after them. As they entered the fringes, the wind began to howl as fresh snow started to fall.

It was Sandy who first commented on a noise within the wind. Faint, but definitely there if one listened intently. 'Where is that sound coming from?'

Janice hushed and took note. 'It sounds like far-off laughter,' she whispered nervously. 'Like children in a nursery.'

Each woman wanted to take a step back but the high-pitched singing seemed to be coming closer from within the depths of the wood. It was uncanny but neither of them could leave. They were compelled to stand and discover what might be coming towards them – afraid and charmed at the same time.

'*La, la, la. La, la, la.*'

They were able to clasp hands for comfort, the only movement they could fulfil. Their dread was thinly smothered by a supernatural compulsion to remain.

'It's the infantile laughter. Like Simon spoke of,' whispered Janice. She was trembling with anxious anticipation and knew Sandy was too.

'*La, la, la. La, la, la.*'

'Look!' Sandy gulped, inclining her head towards a far-off tinkle of light amid the forest ferns. 'It's coming closer.'

'*La, la, la. La, la, la.*'

An aurora of mystical, floating light moved within the trees. Gradually the glowing ball came towards them. Within the chanting, they heard other sounds of high-pitched giggling. Enchanted whispers echoed about the woods. Childish words that Janice recognised. Words that Simon had been muttering… 'Stars are dull in night-time skies.' The words were all about them, compelling the women to look around, wondering from where something or someone might appear.

'*La, la, la. La, la, la.*'

They nervously turned back to the approaching orb of light. Beneath it was a moving mound of snow, the phenomenon of light having a magnetic hold over the singularity of the moving white mound. At the head of the moving snow was the sensational sight of flora, the tiny flowers springing up from shoots, growing and blooming into vibrant hues. Then instantly withering and dying in the wake of the moving white mass. All this astonishing vista performing before their spellbound eyes.

The mesmerising ball of light separated, becoming two hovering spheres that glowed independently. The moving snow mound separated too, each white entity following its separated glowing sphere. Slowly the double celestial phenomenon circled either side and closed towards each captivated woman – a giant horseshoe-shaped mound encircling Janice and Sandy. The green shoots and bright flowers continued to grow, wither and die upon the moving white mounds. It was as though two giant moles were burrowing at speed, following the hovering glow, a compelling sight of flora budding and blooming into vibrant and tantalising colours. The women's awe-struck eyes watched the tingling bursts of delight before the eventual dull, greying decay set in and they sank into the spectres' snowy wake. Then each mound of snow and aurora stopped. The wonder lingered before Janice and Sandy. Dazzling flora continued to sway and dance upon each white floral monument, no longer withering in the constant glow. Each ball of radiance continued to hover above. Then slowly the lights dimmed before them as each clutched the other's hand tighter while gasping for nervous breaths of cold air. They were sweating with fear and compelled to witness the strange wonder.

'I can't move,' exclaimed Sandy fearfully. 'What should we do?'

Janice was unable to reply as she watched the dimming glow sink deeper into the flora and snow. The mound swelled before her eyes as she gulped and resigned herself to the mysterious event, she knew each of them was yet to witness. The gorgeous plants swayed to and fro. It was as though the infantile chanting was emitting from the dancing flowers.

'*La, la, la. La, la, la.*'

Suddenly, the plants and snow erupted with a whoosh about them. They were surrounded by a confetti of cascading flower petals and snow. A brief moment of splendour that dumbfounded both. As the glorious brilliance settled, Janice was shocked to see the frame of a small impish boy.

The urchin was crouched upon a slender branch that he gripped with both hands and toes. As he swayed before Janice, she noted his bare torso was oblivious to the winter wind and snow. He was all but naked apart from a small loincloth that looked like layers of frosted and sparkling cobwebs. His face was turned sideways as Janice studied his celestial profile. With spellbound wonder she observed the slender outline of his delicate cheekbones and little, sharply pointed nose. She made out the tip of a small pointed ear protruding from his wavy raven hair, the shining black mane contrasting against his porcelain white skin. With a spasmodic twist, his head suddenly faced her. His big bright-blue eyes and tiny, pin-sized black pupils contained a hypnotic allurement of dark, malicious secrets.

Janice was compelled to stare back into the inquisitive eyes – there was something diabolical and alluring in the impish being. Her heart fluttered with fear. The young man's smiling face was full of menace. He wore his handsome features on an underdeveloped adolescent boy's body. Slowly, the imp's dreadful smile became wide and more prominent, as though intent on some new mischief. The thin lips parted slightly to reveal a small purple forked tongue, then he hissed like a spiteful kitten that was about to pounce. Beautiful and huge transparent dragonfly wings opened out from behind his back. They splayed out proudly, with a matrix of rainbow-coloured veins. Then the proud wings slowly folded down and out of sight. The impish head jerked lopsidedly, like a naughty little boy pondering his intended misbehaviour. Again, a slight spasmodic movement. His pin-sized black pupils nestled within the glazed icy blue of his irises, like a raptor intent upon its prey.

Janice knew by Sandy's fearful grip that a second impish being was before her friend. Presumably, one just like hers. However, both women were too preoccupied by their own supernatural phenomenon to turn. The gorgeous and dreadful blue irises and the delicate tiny black pupils were filled with enchantment. A compelling wonderment that held the observer transfixed.

Janice looked on as her heartbeat quickened. The grinning fairy's smile broadened even more. Then, like a child making infantile gurgles, he chuckled.

'Look, look into my eyes,' the impish being's voice echoed. The sound of a spiteful little boy intent on torment. 'Look into my eyes. They make stars look dull in night-time skies.'

Then with a swift movement, the playful imp's head jerked forward. It was so fast, so exact. Within that dreadful moment, Janice understood Simon's pain. She felt her forsaken heart go out to the fairy as she received a quick – forever smitten, forever lost – kiss!

CHAPTER 14

RAYMOND GETS AN
UNUSUAL REQUEST

Abigail was relieved to receive the text message from Sandy. She and her friend, Janice, would be walking with the dog. Perhaps up to the Little Wood. Now there was only one nagging worry lingering on her mind. It was, of course, Raymond. He would be expecting her to visit the hospital early and was sure he might be a little worried at her absence. Should she try to call his mobile? It was in his locker by his bed, but she thought the hospital didn't like people calling mobiles in the ward. In fact, she was sure this was so.

As Abigail drove out of Ringwood along the forest road, she glanced at her mobile charging on the hands-free set. At that very moment, as though Raymond might have heard her thoughts, she saw his name flash up on the screen with the welcome sound of her phone beeping. She pressed the loudspeaker enthusiastically while carefully turning a bend along the slippery road. Raymond's voice came through, loud and clear.

'Alright, Abigail. I'm sitting in the toilet cubicle. I sneaked the mobile out with me,' he said.

'Perhaps a little more info than necessary? I don't think you have to sneak it out to the toilet, Raymond. Patients are allowed mobiles. The hospital just prefers you not to use them in the ward.'

He gruffly dismissed her mild rebuke, 'I'm feeling a lot better this morning. You'll never guess what else happened last night?'

Abigail took a guess, 'The man in the cottage, close to the Little Wood. You know, the Careful couple. The bloke was admitted with a cut wrist?'

'How the bloody hell did you know that?' he said, feeling she had stolen his element of surprise by batting back a bigger and better surprise.

'Have you got any more of the lemon balm potion in the plastic beaker, the one I put in your bedside locker?'

'Yes,' he replied. 'I've not needed it, Abigail. I don't feel the abandonment anymore. That was a bewitching spell and your counter one from the book blew that fairy spell away. It honestly works. I know you and that Sandy woman think I'm as mad as a box of frogs, but I'm telling the truth. The blooming nurses think I'm an A1 headcase too. I keep telling myself to stop talking about wraith-like fairy creatures in the Little Wood. But, despite my good intentions, something compels me to keep steering the talk to what I saw. I don't know why and I keep scolding myself afterwards when the medical staff walk off not believing a word I have said. I've not had a blooming meltdown since the spell, but I keep insisting that I saw fairies. I have this over-whelming desire to keep reiterating it.'

'Well, you must fight the compulsion, Raymond. Try your best,' Abigail advised earnestly while tra-versing the slow-moving van over the snowy forest lane.

Raymond cleared his throat. 'Also, that thing you recited and wrote down on the paper. It all works. That whole spell bloody well works. And there are strange little creatures that look like fucking fair-ies in the Little Wood. I'm not sodding about. Why did you buy that old book if you didn't believe the spells?'

'Keep your voice down, Raymond, or those self-important-looking people in white coats will be carting you off, my little dear. I do believe there is something that works. I can't say what it is, but we are both in agreement that it worked with Mr Ballantyne now?'

'Yes,' replied Raymond.

'And we are both in agreement that it somehow worked on you. After you had a meltdown on the main road in Lymington?'

'Yes,' he agreed reluctantly, 'I'm going to feel a bit of a duffer walking about in Lymington from now on.'

'I think you already had a reputation anyway, darling,' she added.

'Well, that's not exactly a confidence booster,' he said with a snort.

Abigail was delighted. Their usual banter was back and in full swing. Mocking one another was all part of their little tradition. A state of almost constant camaraderie.

'I know you never worry about other people's opinions. It's not worth trying to convince them otherwise. Not now. So, hold fire trying to persuade them about fairies in the Little Wood. Mr Ballantyne was guilty of doing the same thing.'

'You're a real bag of laughs, you are,' he whispered. 'Why do you think this Simon Careful fella cut his wrist?'

'The exact same reason as you, darling. He is traumatised and has been kissed by a wraith-like spirit. I think Sandy is beginning to entertain the notion of a supernatural problem concerning the Little Wood.'

'Well, it's about blooming time. Mind you, I never believed old Mr Ballantyne when he was alive. Neither did you, for that matter. Even though you bought that book of spells. Even though you recited the very spell to Mr Ballantyne and declared it a placebo effect.'

'So long as it works, for the moment, Raymond. Let's just work on that principle. I still don't want to jump the gun. Now, I need you to do something for me while you're in the hospital.'

For a moment, Raymond went silent before carefully and slowly replying, 'Right. What would that be?'

'Have you still got that incantation I wrote on the paper next to the beaker in your bedside locker?'

'You mean the one you wrote out in case I had another doggy turn. My "do-it-yourself" fairy-kiss recovery kit. A potion in a plastic beaker plus a roughly written spell in Irish Gaelic to recite to myself?'

'Yes, that's the one.'

'Yes,' he replied slowly with a suspicious tone.

'Is the man from the cottage in your ward?'

'No, he's in a single ward next to mine,' Raymond replied.

'I need you to get in there with the beaker and give him a sip of that mixed lemon balm potion. Once he's drunk it start to read out the spell. You can do it quietly. No need to make a song and dance about it. It's a small incantation and takes seconds.'

'It's written in Irish Gaelic. How will I know if I'm pronouncing it right?'

'I've written the actual pronunciation below the Gaelic script.' Abigail continued to drive the people carrier along the main road when she saw a dead raven lying on the snowy verge. Her foot hit the brakes and she screeched to a halt.

'What was that? Are you alright, Abigail?' Raymond sounded very concerned.

'I'm fine. Hold on a few seconds, I have the ingredients for that dispersal spell I was talking about,' she replied and quickly got out of her vehicle. She walked and slipped along the verge and picked up the dead raven. As she stood there holding up the big raven's dead carcass by the talons, a snooty-looking driver in a metallic grey Jaguar XF cruised past and around her battered-up people carrier. As the pristine vehicle passed, the smartly attired business-man gave her a look of disgust. There she stood in her scruffy New Age clobber, holding her roadkill.

In another moment, she had unceremoniously dumped the dead raven on the passenger seat and resumed her conversation with Raymond. 'Are you still there?'

'Of course, I am. What was that all about?' he asked.

'I've got a dead raven. It's roadkill, I think.'

'Well, good for you. I don't mind a pheasant, but I'm drawing the line at carrion. They eat dead rats.'

'I don't mean the roadkill we sometimes eat. You are a silly sod at times,' she said while restarting the vehicle. She pulled off and continued with her journey towards the late Mr Ballantyne's old place.

'What do you want a dead raven for?' he whispered from the confines of his locked lavatory cubicle.

'I told you when you phoned yesterday. I was reading about other fairy spells last night. There're a few to use. A cluster spell that creates a fairy-free protective circumference of over seventy yards. The incantation is in Irish Gaelic again, but the pronunciation is written beside the actual Gaelic spelling. The spell requires a dead carrion bird. A raven, rook, or crow will do. It was a chance find and I'm still thinking these spells from the book can help us further. You need to get to the man from the cottage in his sick bed. This Simon Careful bloke. The one you think doesn't like you.'

'Oh God,' replied Raymond, 'I need this like I need a hole in my head.'

'Oh, come on, Raymond. Get with the programme. This time we've got some people on board with us. Especially Sandy, the lady's a mental health councillor.'

'Oh, that makes me feel so much better,' replied Raymond sarcastically.

'Sandy and I spoke at length on the way home last night. She believes what you saw. At least she believes you believe it and that you're not crazy. She thinks you're sound.'

'What about me being kissed by a fairy? And you think *she* is sound? As in not gullible? Blooming hell! This is getting better by the minute. Or perhaps she's patronising the both of us?'

Abigail dismissed Raymond's concern. She was glad of the morning light even though more snow was beginning to fall. As usual, she was intent upon her journey while speaking to her hands-free mobile.

'Raymond, please just try to get access to the room where Simon Careful is. Just get him to take a small sip of potion from the beaker and then you're home and dry. The incantation is read out by you and it doesn't matter what happens after that.'

'You speak for yourself. I'm thinking of the people in white coats,' he replied.

There was a sudden banging on the door and a caring voice called in. 'Are you alright in there, Mr Cheeseman?'

'Yes, I'm just washing my hands,' he called back. 'I've got to go, Abigail. I could have done without this chore you've laid on me. But I'll give it a try.'

'Oh, dashed well done, Raymond. Once more to the breach, me ol' mucker.' She laughed and turned the car's hands-free off.

Things were falling into place. Abigail couldn't say why but she felt optimistic. Raymond was back to his comical dry sense of humour and their banter was back in full swing. Now for Sandy's new dilemma with her friend Janice. What trials and tribulations lay in wait at the Little Wood?

CHAPTER 15

NELLY TO THE RESCUE

Sandy was on her back, and she slowly sat up from the snow-covered floor amid the excitable commotion of Nelly barking and wraith-like squealing from the diabolical little impish creatures. She was shocked but gathering her confused wits. The supernatural enchantment had been broken just in time.

She remembered the host fairy had appeared before her amid the cascading snowflakes and flower petals. The impish lad had thick, wavy white hair and was swaying up and down upon a branch beside Janice's host sprite with the raven hair. Each imp had small pointed ears sticking out of their short, tangled locks, with smooth, handsome little faces. The white-haired little winged wraith was about to leap forward and kiss Sandy. The creature's face was beaming with glee, like a lizard about to lunge for the telling strike. The same way Janice's raven-haired fairy host had got her, a split second earlier. Then everything had become confused.

Nelly, growling, snarling and barking had leapt between Sandy and the white-haired impish lad to stand by Janice. Nelly wanted to protect her much-loved mistress from the raven-haired rascal. In the course of the mutt's action she had inadvertently saved Sandy from the forever-smitten kiss by knocking her backwards. The mesmerising spell of her fairy assailant was broken.

Nelly had bitten the raven-haired fairy boy, who had kissed Janice, her sharp teeth snapping several times along the strange creature's thin little arm. The impish boy had squealed and hissed while falling wounded from the bobbing tree branch. The green leaves immediately began to decompose and break away from the branches.

The wicked sprite yelped again and twisted away in the white hail, his transparent wings crumpling in the crushed snow. Quickly, the creature got to his tiny feet and shook his wings, the wet sleet falling away. His naked and anaemic torso heaved up and down. Small but well-formed stomach muscles rippled as the quaint and wicked little thing stood there in a small, thick cobwebbed loincloth.

About the urchin's tiny toes, small flora began to grow. The brattish thing took another step back and the same flora began to wither and die. New tiny flowers instantly began to grow about the creature's new standing position.

The little urchin stared down at his arm. It was bleeding. The diabolical little thing looked up from his wound at Nelly. The dog was standing by her fallen mistress with her teeth bared angrily and snarling.

The fairy boy's porcelain face contorted into a look of shock and anger. Standing like an infant's uncanny doll, it bared its small, sharp-looking fangs, and its tiny forked tongue hissed like an angry snake. For a moment it seemed to defy Nelly. But the angry dog was having none of the impudent sprite's threats. She took another threatening step forward and growled her warning.

The boyish imp retreated another step. More flora decayed in the small vacant footprint. The little gremlin was angrily coming to grips with his nasty surprise. But the extraordinary little urchin tried once again. He gritted his fangs and hissed spitefully. His small naked torso was oblivious to the cold winter's snow and the thick, shredded cobweb-like garment, around his lower waist, did little to combat such cold. It barely covered his impish modesty. The second, white-haired scallywag was dressed in equally skimpy, glittering cobweb attire. It moved closer to stand beside his companion in mischief.

Nelly's teeth remained on display. Her ferocious snarl threatened more retribution as she moved aggressively closer to the little insidious fairy boys. For a moment, the little supernatural beings had stopped retreating. They adopted a threatening stance in order to stand their ground. Each fairy's bare feet were fixed in the snow with a new mass of tiny flora growing and blooming about their standing base. The blue of each wicked boy's eyes blazed like a malicious lizard intent on a predatory strike. A new calculating malice drank in the dog's form, tiny black pupils like pinpricks in a swirling azure. Two little heads spasmodically turned from side to side as though contemplating the next move. Transparent dragonfly wings splayed behind their backs threateningly, fluttering in an agitated manner.

The dog creature before them could not be entranced the way humans could. The raven-haired fairy spitefully hissed again as the white-haired wraith did the same in a duet of disapproval. The two fairies remained together facing the black Labrador, their little forked tongues slipping in and out quickly the way reptiles do.

Nelly sprang forward and attacked again! Suddenly, quick and ferocious. The wraith-like boys recoiled amid fearful, high-pitched screams. The dog's sharp fangs ripped into bare flesh and leg muscle. More blood and further irrepressible, wailing fear. Fear a dog could sense and fear Nelly used to her advantage as she leapt at the second fairy with white hair, biting and ripping more flesh and smelling more strange blood. The uncanny taste and smell amid her snarling pack-protecting anger.

The routed and terrified imps leapt backwards and dived into the settling snowdrift outside of the woods. Two mounds of white flurry beat a hasty retreat, quickly moving out onto the heathland and into the fresh snowfall, the usual cascade of flora blooming instantly and then withering and dying on each moving mound's wake. Vibrant life followed by sad death in mere moments as the hidden uncanny creatures burrowed further away from the scene of attack.

All about, in the immediate woodland vicinity, Sandy watched in spellbound disbelief. The blood drops on the snow played host to the growth of short-lived flowers that grew the same way as on the retreating snow mounds. The sad, withering petals dying before her very eyes.

'They literally buried themselves in the snow, Janice. Did you see that?' Sandy stammered in shocked awe. She watched as the mounds retreated into the snowfall.

Janice started to whisper incoherently. She raised herself to a sitting position and looked up to the snow falling between the bare branches of the woods. 'Such wicked little things. How could they be so nasty?'

'Janice,' Sandy called in alarm.

'Now I know what they did to my Simon. You wicked, beastly little things,' she sobbed and began to break down as tears of utter sorrow ran down her troubled face.

Nelly was still barking out on the heathland into the snowfall and in the direction the fairies had retreated.

'Good girl, Nelly!' Sandy called as she walked over to Janice. She was in a traumatised state looking at her splayed fingers that she held up before her eyes. 'Janice, are you alright?' cried Sandy in concern.

Janice whispered again, 'Such lovely and wicked little things. Why have they left us? What did the little loves do that for?'

Sandy clasped Janice and pulled her arm over her shoulder. Slowly she guided her staggering friend out of the woods and onto the heathland. Out into the swirling blizzard. She called back to the black Labrador, 'Come on, Nelly. We must get back.'

Nelly yelped once and then began to whine as she followed the two women into the snow out onto the white-blanketed heath.

Janice could only just about stand with Sandy's aid. She was distraught and crying like a little lost child – like she was in an uncontrollable state of bereavement.

'It's alright, Janice,' said Sandy soothingly as she struggled down the heath in the blustery blizzard, desperately trying to hold Janice up. 'We must get you back to the house.'

'Why did the nasty little things leave us?' Janice whispered incoherently.

Sandy turned to the dog and called, 'Nelly, keep watch and follow. Watch them, Nelly. Watch out for the little bastards. They might be back and there must be more of them. I don't think they're finished yet.'

Nelly barked a quick acknowledgement. The loyal mutt knew what was wanted as she dutifully walked alongside the two women, whining and snarling while looking through the blizzard at the white heathland. She was like a moving sentinel guarding Janice and Sandy from the unearthly harm that was watching and waiting. The battle was only just beginning.

CHAPTER 16

RAYMOND MUST FIND A WAY

'This is a real peach of an ask, Abigail,' Raymond whispered to himself, while imagining Abigail was somewhere in his mind listening. He was in one of his sulking moods. The sort of disposition his old partner Abigail had a special little saying for.

He could just picture an imaginary Abigail saying, 'You've got a right old cob on. Snap out of it!'

And so, Raymond allowed his surreal and imaginary Abigail to act out what his very real Abigail would probably say. It worked, and gradually, Raymond started to look at the obstacles before him. Somehow, he had to formulate a way of getting past the big ward sister's sharp scrutiny and into Simon Careful's single ward. Then he had to administer the lemon balm potion to a sleeping Simon Careful followed by the counter spell incantation that would withdraw the fairy-kiss spell.

'Blimey,' he muttered to his imaginary Abigail. 'I'll start blurting this fairy tale stuff out if I'm cornered. I know I will. My cakehole will start motoring when I'm put on the spot.'

Don't get cornered then, and grit your teeth, replied the imaginary Abigail inside his head.

He leaned back in the visitor's chair next to his hospital bed and surveyed all about him. Outside the ward, he could see along the corridor to a reception desk. At this particular reception area, sat a tall and slightly rotund lady. A formidable-looking ward sister of about six foot four in a dark blue uniform, her blond hair pulled back in a tight, thick ponytail.

Blimey, she looks like an impressive piece of work, he thought within his mind's eye, where his imaginary Abigail stood.

Every now and then, the intimidating profile of the ward sister would look up from her work to observe her section of the hospital. All that was before her. To the front, for starters, where the intercom-system fire doors were – they led out to the main passageway. Also, the very strip of inner-ward corridor where Raymond's small side ward was. Then the ward sister would glance to her right and then her left. There she sat, at the T-junction of corridors. When satisfied, she resumed with her paperwork. The overall section of corridors with its various side wards was her little domain and she was in charge.

'Blast and bollocks!' he muttered to himself. 'There she is, sitting on her throne like the large-breasted queen of the castle.'

The buxom lady had the aura of a person who was in charge. She wore a stern look of assurance. Confident in the abilities of her power and, perhaps, someone who would not suffer fools gladly. Raymond felt a little nervous about the last aspect of his judgement concerning the ward sister. For some reason he heard Abigail's voice saying, 'She will not suffer fools gladly, so be careful.'

'Bloody cheek,' he whispered to himself and looked around nervously in case another patient might have heard him.

Raymond kept up his crafty observation, hoping to spot a weakness. Alas, there was nothing he could find that remotely appeared weak. The rather plump lady with her thick blond plait and huge breasts seemed a very stalwart and formidable individual indeed.

'She'd frighten the life out of most men,' he said to his imaginary Abigail.

Including thin lanky men of your calibre, Raymond, replied his make-believe Abigail. He wished she'd refrain from being so flippant.

The ward sister looked a little overworked and seemed abrupt when speaking to other nurses in light-blue uniforms, but he noticed she seemed a little more respectful of another nurse in a royal blue outfit. Perhaps she was something a little higher in rank? Raymond could no longer work out what rankings other hospital staff were. He could only assume.

Raymond suddenly stiffened, alert to a new development. One younger carer, in a light-blue uniform, had pushed the medication trolly up close to the reception desk. No doubt, about to do the rounds. The young nurse was interrupted by the ward sister, obviously instructed to do something that required her immediate attention. What it was, Raymond couldn't say because he was spying on them from his chair at a distance, through the open ward door. The unknown instruction had created a circumstance of the young nurse leaving the vicinity to attend the unknown matter. Raymond noticed the wheeled trolly was abandoned by the admin desk. It contained the medicine rounds for various patients. Surely, Simon Careful's medicine would be on the trolly. If only he could get close enough to have a look. There would be written names on moulded capsule trays and plastic cups. He had noticed that patients' names were always written on all the beakers and moulded pill holders.

Raymond nonchalantly got up out of his bedside chair and ambled out of his ward and along the corridor towards the reception desk. He chanced a glance inside the single ward where Simon Careful was in a sedated sleep. There were monitors and drip feeds, which made Raymond wince at the memory of his being taken out. So far so good. No one was chastising him to go back to bed. Perhaps the ward sister at the desk didn't know he should be confined to his bed for a little longer. Or maybe they didn't mind him walking about provided they could see him.

'Can I help you?' The buxom ward sister had looked up and spotted him.

Raymond saw a small bookcase by the wheeled trolly. His quick thinking kicked in as he asked, 'Am I allowed to look at those books? May I borrow one to read if I choose?'

She looked down at them and then replied, 'That's what they're there for. Take a look. I'm sure there'll be something for you.'

'Thank you.' Raymond smiled as he walked towards the bookshelf bypassing the medicine trolly. He glanced at the various small beakers and noticed plastic cups in holders with pills. There were names against wards and the cups with small plastic moulds containing pills. Simon Careful's name was spotted immediately. A cup with a top, containing a pre-prepared liquid and some pills in the small gully mould.

The severe-looking ward sister went back to her work on her computer screen. Raymond pretended to look at the various books while covertly glancing at the big ward sister. He was searching for a way to get Simon Careful's liquid medicine. He needed to tip it away and then pour some of the lemon balm potion into the container instead of the prescribed medicine. The whole way of getting him to drink the liquid was before him. He just needed clear access to the tiny beaker and a way to dispose of the medicine under the nose of the formidable, curvaceous ward sister.

Blimey, I bet she could do her husband some damage, he thought. *Sod that for a lark.*

He was assuming she was a ward sister though he'd never heard anyone address her as such. The NHS dress code was different from his younger days and he couldn't always work out the difference in ranks. Or even if hospitals had these old ranks anymore. He quietly scolded himself for watching too many retro sixties *Carry On* comedy films where nurses seemed to wear skirts and dresses. It was all trouser suits in this more modern day.

Suddenly, Raymond noticed the young nurse further along the corridor beckoning to the ward sister who was engrossed in her computer. This was a chance he couldn't afford to lose.

'Excuse me, lady, I think that nurse is waving for you,' he said, thinking the big lady looked the complete battleaxe. A kindly and well-intentioned woman, no doubt, but still an awe-inspiring and intolerant-looking beast.

'Oh, Christ,' she hissed under her breath as she stood up and ambled along the corridor to attend the need of the younger nurse.

Raymond, seizing the opportunity before him, took a quick look around and grabbed Simon Careful's small beaker of liquid medicine from the trolly. There was a wastepaper bin by the desk with a few screwed-up pieces of paper inside. He removed the beaker top and tipped the liquid medicine into the bin. Again, he glanced about slyly as he removed the lemon balm beaker from his pocket. He lifted the container's lid, then proceeded to tip a small measure of the mixed lemon balm contents into Simon Careful's medicine beaker. He replaced the lid and put it back from where he'd taken it. He also secured and put his lemon balm potion back into his dressing-gown pocket and went back to looking at the books. He developed a rather noticeable, pleased with himself, swagger as his mind searched within for his invented Abigail mental-support system. And then he spoke to her.

'The good old bloke hormones are bubbling to the surface. I'm the dashing secret agent fulfilling his daring mission.'

Oh, Sean Connery, eat your heart out, scolded his imaginary Abigail. *You've done very well, my little sausage. Now there's still another part of the task to complete.*

As usual, even the imaginary Abigail brought him down to earth as did the real Abigail on so many occasions.

'That's right,' he told himself, coming down from his feel-good fantasy. 'I'm the sausages bloke.'

He pulled out a Minette Walters novel titled *The Shape of Snakes* and heard the ward sister's voice call to him. He jumped in shock.

'That's a splendid story,' she called with a more approving smile on her face. The big lady walked along the corridor towards the desk area. Her huge breasts swinging from side to side in a threatening manner.

Raymond gulped anxiously and forced a smile. He waved the paperback nervously. 'I've read a few of her novels before. They're very good.'

The younger nurse was with the ward sister, smiling approvingly. Whatever task they'd been attending seemed to have been quickly resolved – in a satisfactory manner judging by the new mood of both of the hospital workers.

'Really, that's nice to know,' replied the big ward sister approvingly. 'I'm a big fan. What ones have you read?'

'Oh, *The Sculptress*, *The Dark Room* and *Acid Row*,' he replied, confident of the ward sister's approval.

Her eyes widened with appreciative pleasure. 'Oh, indeed! If you enjoyed those, I'm certain you'll enjoy *The Shape of Snakes*. In my humble opinion, it's her best. And let's be honest, with all of Minette Walters very good novels this book is up against some stiff competition.'

Raymond struggled with the thought of anything concerning the ward sister being humble. He just couldn't imagine her doing anything modest at all. Also, the stiff competition aspect, of her opinion, had a limp meaning in his shrinking masculine outlook. He'd gone from John Wayne's *Stagecoach* movie character to Donald Meek's in the blink of an eye.

The ward sister's imposing figure came closer, bearing down upon him like an affectionate elephant. Raymond felt compelled to act confidently and willed himself to assertively stand his ground, like a confident man, oozing with fresh and hard-nosed masculinity.

'Well that sounds like a fabulous recommendation. I'll start this today if I may?' He quickly dismissed the idea of hard-nosed masculinity and decided that brains were the better part of valour on this one occasion.

The ward sister looked down at his mere skinny six-foot-one inch frame with a big beaming smile and replied, 'Enjoy!'

The younger nurse smiled too as she wheeled the trolly along the corridor to start her medicine rounds.

Raymond smiled nervously and retreated back to his ward from where he could formulate his next approach. The second part of his Abigail-inflicted task.

Good lord! he scolded her in his mind's eye. *You certainly squash the best out of me.*

He sighed to himself and sat back in his bed-side armchair to contemplate further. He needed to recite the spell in Irish Gaelic once Simon had sipped the draft. The troubled man would be free of the torment in minutes. This, he knew from his own experience and that of the late Mr Ballantyne. He was grateful his bed was the first on the right when entering the ward – it was the perfect observation spot for the next part of his plan. A plan he'd been making up in an ad hoc, devil-may-care manner. His head swayed slightly as he revelled in his own creative ingenuity. Away from the ward sister, his masculine fever had returned with great aplomb. There, in the armchair for visitors, he imagined the Hollywood film stars had nothing on him.

'John Wayne, Clint Eastwood, or Arnold Schwarzenegger,' he muttered to himself and then added, 'Go eat your bleeding hearts out! Raymond Cheeseman is the real bloody deal, mate.'

Slow down, sausage, said the fantasy Abigail's mental cushion.

'Gate crasher!' he whispered back.

Don't get carried away, sausage.

'Forget your Predator, Arnie. The ward sister's the real deal,' he whispered, living the dream. He was in the adventure of his life. 'Who needs ambition when it all just falls in your lap? Besides, ambition is in the hands of a lot of rather pushy people,' he bemoaned, having another look at the fearsome ward sister.

He watched as the big-breasted lady began calling out instructions to two more nurses. A harsh, frowning face that suggested it wouldn't endure inefficiency.

'I better keep well out of her way,' he whispered to himself. 'I'll just sit here and watch. I'll know when the nurse doing the medicine rounds comes back along the corridor. I'll know when she goes into Simon's isolated ward, and I'll know when she closes the door and leaves. I can sneak in and have complete privacy to read the spell out. In Gaelic. That's still a big ask but somehow, I must do it.'

Raymond sighed at the prospect. He turned and looked out of the hospital's big windows. Outside, the snow was cascading down but it was lost on him in the warm ward. He was lost in his thoughts, unsure about this final part, especially where pronunciation in Gaelic was concerned. Raymond raised an eyebrow and opened the Minette Walters novel. He began to read.

CHAPTER 17

ESCAPE IN THE SNOWSTORM

The snowstorm was getting stronger as Sandy struggled to hold Janice. Nelly, the faithful black Labrador, was trying to lead the way through the blizzard. Everywhere was a total whiteout with cascading white snowflakes swirling and falling. Within the swishing bluster came the faint sound that would surely grow louder.

'*La, la, la. La, la, la.*'

'They're getting ready to come at us again,' shouted Sandy amid the snowstorm.

Janice's head hung limply. She barely managed to take any steps – depending heavily on her friend for support. Slowly she raised her tired head and smiled as the snowflakes hit her freckled face. She opened her tired eyes and replied, 'Oh, the wicked little darlings are coming back for us. They must never leave us again – never!'

'You mustn't talk like that, Janice,' Sandy scolded and jerked her friend upright as she got a stronger and better grip. 'Come on now, Janice. We must follow Nelly.'

They were halfway down the slope of the open heathland. A heath that was buried in a blanket of white, drifting flurry. It was getting deeper by the moment. The complete whiteout was being fed with more cascading snow, a white deluge flying and landing everywhere about them. It was difficult to make out the path when it was completely gone. Only the snow-covered heath clusters helped as Sandy laboured around the mounds, desperately clasping Janice's arm over her own shoulder, her other hand firmly gripping around her friend's waist. Half dragging the woman and sometimes encouraging her to take unsteady steps.

'Keep going, Janice! We mustn't give up. Not now. We're halfway to the Side Wood. Just a little way now. Just a little more effort,' Sandy encouraged.

Nelly continued to lead the way and seemed to have a stronger sense of direction. The black Labrador scouted ahead and then kept turning to bark. A canine request to follow.

'There, Nelly is leading the way,' Sandy called amid the robust snow.

'Such wicked little things,' Janice cried out, mentally demoralised as though something emotionally precious had been taken from her.

The faint song of torment increased in volume as it filtered through the flurry of white flakes. Janice held her head up and groaned. Almost as though delighted by the ominous sound.

'*La, la, la. La, la, la.*'

'Oh,' Janice called hopefully, like an excited child, 'they're coming back for us. Perhaps they will not desert me? Not now? Not if they know how much I care for them?'

'Come on now, Janice. We must keep going. Now is not the time to give up. We must get to your home as soon as possible,' called Sandy over the blustering snowy weather and the din of infantile singing that seemed to be growing louder by the second.

'*La, la, la. La, la, la.*'

Nelly began to bark excitedly out towards the flanking snowy heathland. The black-haired mutt was getting agitated about something.

'What is it, Nelly? Are they after us again?' Sandy asked as she struggled past the Labrador.

The mutt began to whine her displeasure. Nelly barked again and then followed after Sandy, the strange lady who struggled with her lethargic and injured mistress. The dog knew why her mistress was in a very distressed state. It was the strange little people creatures that emerged from the flowering snow. The germ-free ones that touched without touching. The strange little things that had no smell. Nelly kept stopping to look out at the snowy flanks. Something was moving parallel with them and it was getting closer. It had no smell but it was touching and feeling through the white flurry.

Sandy called back as she struggled on with Janice, 'Come on, Nelly. There's a good girl. Keep up now.'

Nelly complied and began to run towards her. Knowing the urgency of the situation. Aware of the need to protect her mistress and the lady who was helping her. They were a pack and they were in danger from strange, trespassing little creatures that were void of scent.

At the same moment, Sandy heard the mound of moving snow out on the path's flank. From the very direction Nelly had been observing. Even within the haze of the swirling blizzard, Sandy could make out the colourful flora growing and blooming and then withering and dying upon the moving mound's wake – a surfing movement of bursting colour rolling towards them.

'Here they come again,' called Sandy as she hurried onwards, supporting Janice in her weary state.

Nelly charged out into the deepening snow of the heathland. Straight at the approaching mound of blooming and withering flora – instant growth, life and death on moving snow. The determined dog's snarling aggression was ferocious and her intention was for a violent confrontation.

As though the hidden and burrowing wraiths could see the brutish mutt before them, the mound veered off and away from the group.

'A momentary respite! Well done, Nelly,' called Sandy. 'Come on, girl. Follow us now. We need you more than ever. Come now, Nelly,' called Sandy as she realised the uncanny enemy had developed a healthy fear of the wonderful black Labrador bitch – an animal defending her besieged pack.

Again, Nelly complied and followed after the two struggling women. She moved past Sandy and Janice and made for the woodland by the side of the house. All would find some form of sanctuary there. A place of safety. For a while at least.

As Sandy struggled with Janice towards the perimeter of the Side Wood, she noticed irregular areas along the edge of the trees through the hazy swirl. There were unnatural patches of green foliage, vibrant green clusters in their mid-summer bloom – absolute full maturity in mid-winter and during a potent snowstorm. The infernal infantile din was coming from every direction now.

'*La, la, la. La, la, la.*'

Sandy blinked and peered more intently. Then gulped in dismay. She recognised the distant supernatural forms. Little wraith-like beings perched amid the distant branches, bobbing within clusters of equally unusual green leaves, the winter snowstorm raging all about. The insidious little supernatural beings all emitting a cacophony of excited chanting.

'*La, la, la. La, la, la.*'

Janice raised herself temporarily. 'Oh, the wicked little things are coming for us. Will they stay this time?'

Her head dropped once again and Sandy was forced to readjust her hold on the failing form of Janice before trying to proceed.

Janice continued to mumble, 'Little humanoid creatures with dragonfly wings. Did you see their clothes? Their shredded and scanty cobwebbed garments? Cobwebs to cover their slight forms. Impish little things bobbing up and down upon the moving branches amid this swirling blizzard.'

'Come on, Janice,' encouraged Sandy. 'You must grit your teeth and keep trying to walk with me. Don't give up, Janice? Please keep trying.'

'*La, la, la. La, la, la.*'

'Horrible little darlings. Little grinning groups of crouching mischief. Waiting excitedly for the approach of us, their guests – us, the reluctant visitors – their new prey. Such wicked, horrid little things,' spat Janice as she tried to keep walking while aided by her devoted friend.

'They'll try to surround us once we're inside the woodland. But we must try to get through to your house, Janice. We can't stay out here in the blizzard.' Sandy realised the rascally little creatures were anticipating their arrival and entry to the Side Wood.

Nelly was whining and looking up at the scene too as she led the way to the woods. She suddenly halted to look up at the strange lady, Sandy, who was struggling with her lethargic and sleepy mistress – a forlorn and emotionally devastated person. Someone lost to them.

Sandy stopped too, just for a moment and adjusted her hold once again on her dejected friend, Janice. Then she spoke to the sad-looking dog, 'Their concealment is betrayed, Nelly. That's because their very presence entices vibrant green foliage to grow. Look, it grows about their immediate proximity. Such filthy and diabolical little urchins.'

Nelly barked twice as though she had a rudimentary understanding of what was said. Then she continued and led the way into the wood with Sandy and Janice desperately following. The noise of the blizzard dropped and the snowfall lost all intensity amid the trees. But the infantile chanting became louder and closer.

'*La, la, la. La, la, la.*'

Janice looked up with elated eyes. Tears of joy rolled down her freckled cheeks. Her melancholy sadness dissolved.

'They've come back for me,' she called in awe and delight.

'No, Janice, you can't go to them,' scolded Sandy as she forcefully pulled Janice on and deeper into the woods, taking paths where there was no tell-tale green foliage.

Nelly began to bark at Janice too. Somehow the mutt was aware of her mistress's vulnerability.

Within the woods, the howling snowstorm's noise continued to recede. But the new hullabaloo of infantile giggling erupted with frightful glee. It was crammed with wicked delight and coming from every direction. A continuous, tormenting harmony of excited chanting.

'*La, la, la. La, la, la.*'

'That giggling is getting closer,' Sandy shouted as panic began to set in. Fear was growing within her chest and she could feel Janice weakly struggling to be free of her restraining grip and the arm about her waist.

'Let me go, Sandy, please?' Janice cried.

'I can't, Janice. We need to get back to the house.'

Nelly ran towards an area of woodland where growing leaf foliage had suddenly bloomed. She was barking and snarling aggressively. Instantly the green began to wither and die, a sign of the unseen wicked imps retreating from the position. The faithful dog quickly returned, whining her displeasure of their situation, knowing she had her pack to protect, her dog instincts kicking in.

'Good girl, Nelly,' stuttered Sandy as she tried to compose herself and tightened her grip on Janice.

Janice remained in a weak and yearning state. The forever-smitten fairy kiss had left her useless and unable to make reason of anything except the uncanny feeling of loss. A deep emotional sense of bereavement on an intensity she could not begin to explain.

'Such wicked little things,' she sobbed, while allowing herself to be led through the woods by Sandy's forceful and protective intention.

Nelly continued to protectively circle the two women, barking at the trees and the engulfing cacophony of childish giggling amid ominous, high-pitched chanting.

'*La, la, la. La, la, la.*'

Every now and then, Nelly would break away from the slow, struggling couple and charge out barking towards a patch of growing green leaves. Then she would quickly retreat back to guard Sandy and Janice as the leaves began to turn brown and quickly die.

'Good girl, Nelly. We're doing well. I think we might get—'

Sandy stopped talking as foliage began to instantly grow all about them. A surrounding circle of vibrant green suddenly growing to a fullness of bloom. Leaves in winter on bushes and in the trees. Nelly whined her displeasure. There were too many patches of green to attack. She backed defensively into Sandy and Janice.

'Stay by us, Nelly,' stuttered Sandy as she felt the hairs on her shaking arms stand on end. The chanting had gone and the giggling had subdued to hissing whispers, as though the hidden imps had the group exactly where they wanted them to be. Perhaps the strange little fairy folk would come leaping at them out of the greenery. They were surrounded. Sandy knew it and so did the dog, Nelly. Janice was week and exhausted – their dire circumstance was too much for her.

'The gorgeous little things are here for me,' she whispered. 'They'll rush out in a moment. You'll not mind once they kiss you. Just don't let them leave afterwards. The hurt is too much to bear. They did it to my poor Simon. Now I understand what happened to him. If we could only get him back here, I'm sure he'd feel better.'

Then, from out of the green foliage they slowly emerged. From behind bushes and trees, the little scantily clad impish people took a first step into the wooded clearing. They were about three to three and a half foot tall. Each imp was very thin and slight in stature. Male fairies with short wavy hair and little pointed ears poking through tangled locks of varying colours – fair, ginger, raven and snow-white. Delicate-looking dragonfly wings flickered up and out from behind their backs, spectral colours about the vein tributaries of the transparent, winged membrane. They had young, porcelain white faces with big blue eyes and tiny pin-sized black pupils. Their heads twitched spasmodically and bent to the side like reptiles, intent on their prey. Each male had a shredded cobweb-woven cloth covering his modesty. The cold didn't seem to affect them in any way – they were completely resilient to it.

Behind the males, were the female wraiths. Almost the same, apart from longer locks cascading down past their shoulders. And their sparkling cobweb garments were shredded frocks that covered their bodies from the neck down to the upper thighs of their bare legs. In a strange and compelling way, they were elegant – beautiful and wicked at the same time. A complete contrast. A hypocritical sight of diabolical enticement. A surrounding crowd of wicked little fairies that were real.

'It's like a scene from a story book but this is no fantasy,' whispered Sandy.

Her heart skipped several beats. She gulped and looked at their bare feet in the snow. Creeping phlox flowers quickly grew and bloomed about each imp's little toes. As each creature slowly moved, the purple, pink and white flora instantly withered away.

'Creeping phlox can't grow in a forest,' Sandy muttered in shock. She was waiting for the vile and pretty little things to rush them. 'Creeping phlox needs sunlight. What are these horrid little things that make plants grow so quickly in any conditions?'

'They radiate an aurora,' muttered Janice appreciatively. 'They are lovable little roguish things. Such naughty little dears.'

Sandy guessed there were about forty or more of the impish creatures now slowly circling them. Upon the floor she noted a thick branch about the size of a club.

'Any moment, Nelly,' Sandy whispered, looking to the dog. She let Janice's lethargic form slide from her grip and fall away upon the forest floor. Then she slowly bent down and picked up a thick branch, her last resort. She took a stance and held her branch like a club. Nelly was snarling beside her and holding her own battle-ready stance. Together they braced themselves for the rush that must surely come.

Upon the forest floor before them, Janice muttered once more, 'Such wicked little things, such lovely little nasty darlings.'

A moment of quietness. The calm before the storm. Sandy held her breath in anticipation as the fairy mites took tentative first steps towards the group.

Sandy gritted her teeth and took a practice swing of her branch club, while Nelly growled and bared her teeth at the cautiously approaching fairy horde.

'Any second now, Nelly,' whispered Sandy.

Unexpectedly, there was a swishing sound coming from above. Something hurtling through the air. A dead raven fell into the area between them and the confronting wall of advancing fairies. The dead bird's talons were tied to a brick that splattered upon the forest clearing with an unceremonious thud. Unrecognisable Gaelic words were called out. A mystic Irish spell that seemed to leave each fairy rascal looking in open-mouthed wonder. The incantation stopped and a supernatural force of distorted air fanned out from the dead raven like ripples in a still pond. The scallywag fairy creatures hissed and backed away into the green foliage. The vegetation immediately began to turn brown – a sign of fairy absence and abandonment.

'Oh no,' cried Janice as she rolled onto her back, 'the sadness of it all makes things wither and die.'

'Oh, my word, that was very close, Sandy,' said Abigail as she came out of the wood and into the clearing. She was clutching her long-handled cloth shopping bag that contained her treasured book *Witchcraft – Spells and Potions*. The strangely clad

New Age lady went to her dead raven and borrowed brick, bent down and picked up her new, treasured possessions.

'That was a close-run thing,' said Sandy. A tone of gratitude in her strained voice.

'I can use this again. I think we may have to,' added Abigail.

'What was that you did, Abigail?' asked Sandy. She looked about for signs of green leaf.

'It was another anti-fairy spell. One of the very spells I spoke of on the phone. As you can see it works. I think they all work.'

Sandy was lifting Janice to her feet as Abigail came forward to help.

'She was kissed by one of those things up in the Little Wood. They were about to complete their work. I was saved by Nelly. She bit one and chased them off on several occasions.'

Abigail looked down at Nelly and said, 'Dashed well done, Nelly.'

Nelly replied with a gentle yelp of acknowledgement and then whined impatiently. The dog wanted to be back at the house.

'I know we'll need to get back to the house but first I must use the enchantment on both of you. You'll need to drink the mixed lemon balm potion and allow me to recite the words. Your friend will heal very quickly. I need to do it right now, there's no time to lose and I think those little creatures will have another go at us very soon. But their spell-binding kisses won't work once our counter spell is cast. The late Mr Ballantyne often said as much. Though we never believed the poor man.'

Abigail pulled out a beaker with a plastic lid from her long rainbow-coloured cardigan.

Sandy raised an eyebrow. 'You look like the complete Earth mother, a New Age warrior with your lemon balm concoction, your book of spells plus your dead raven and tethered brick. Well, perhaps not the brick.'

Abigail nodded in her usual geeky way. 'Well the brick helps to throw the dead raven. Tethered to said brick, it's easier to aim the brick and let the tethered raven follow.'

'I see,' replied Sandy, chuckling. 'Must we really drink that? Have you already taken it?'

'I have, Sandy, and it's very important we get this out of the way now. Please indulge me here and now. It's worth it and I'm most anxious we get this part done. I feel we might still need to defend against another attack once inside the house. Evidently fairies take some time before they realise when a counter spell is working against them. They will get spiteful if they can't get their way. They'll bite and scratch.'

Janice looked afraid. 'What sort of spiteful do you mean? Are you sure they'll attack again?'

'They can bite with their sharp little fangs and act like bad-tempered little children. They're incredibly spoilt little things and they'll resent losing your friend's affections. For some reason they covert the affectionate misery they inflict on an abandoned subject. There will be a bigger effort to claim your friend according to the spell book I've been reading. It'll not do them any good. Once the counter spell is cast, they'll never be able to infect your friend again or any of us in future. But they will invade the privacy of the house at night. They'll want to place some form of standard in the property. They may have already done it. I need to do another spell to counter this potential threat too.'

'So, you mean these little impish things aren't giving up yet?' Sandy peered around her nervously while propping Janice up against her.

Abigail moved forward and lifted the beaker to Sandy's lips. 'Just the merest of sips. That's all it takes,' she said.

Sandy complied and winced at the horrid taste. Then she helped as Janice was mad to take a sip.

'Urgh!' Janice gagged. 'That was disgusting.'

Abigail then pulled out her piece of crumpled paper and recited her spell, '*Bí imithe mites Domhan. Fill ar ais ar do fhearann.*'

'Has your mobile gone offline too, by the way? Mine had no signal as we ran out of the Little Wood,'

Sandy asked, hoping they might be able to make an emergency call.

'It has, Sandy. I noticed it on my van's Bluetooth when I arrived at the cottage. It also wasn't receiving a signal when I got out of the van and checked. I was going to call you, but…'

Janice suddenly stood upright and said, 'Oh my God! That was an awful experience.'

'You're recovered?' asked Sandy.

Janice's eyes widened and she turned to Abigail. 'Thank you so much. That has worked. Will it last? Can my husband have some?'

'Of course, my dear. He's in the same area of hospital wards as my Raymond. Even as we speak, he's doing the same thing to help your husband. He may be trying to call us now. But something has blocked the mobile phone signal. I'm wondering if it's all part of the enchantment of the surrounding area. It would make sense.'

'I think we should get back to the house and consider what to do next,' advised Janice, gathering her wits.

'What, not to the cars and off?' asked Sandy.

In unison, Abigail and Janice replied, 'No!'

'Why not?' Sandy asked.

Abigail spoke, 'There's also a protective spell for the house. I did this for Mr Ballantyne too. But for the new owners, I must do it again.'

Janice sighed. 'I know you might think I'm being irrational, Sandy. But I have no intention of being driven out of this home. There is something of a protective resilience in that potion you gave me. How do I know that?'

'Because there is no devotion to the fairies now. Only an anger and a desire to protect. But we must win this right and they will try to breach the house defences.'

'So, it's back to my house then and the siege that will surely come?'

'That is correct, young lady,' replied Abigail. 'Oh, and by the way. I have several of these for defending the house. I presume we are going to be inside for the next attack? They will come again if my understanding is correct.'

Abigail pulled her long-handled canvas bag from her shoulder. It was packed with a multitude of things. She searched within and pulled out three old plastic washing-up liquid, squirting containers. Upon the side in cheap bubble lettering were the words, 'Bargain Shopper Washing Up Liquid'.

'Bargain Shopper?' Janice said, looking a little snooty.

'I suppose the Fairy product might have been more appropriate but it's the actual container we need,' replied Abigail.

'I presume the washing-up liquid is spent and you have another concoction inside each of these?' asked Sandy, taking one of the plastic bottles.

'It's a concoction of lemon balm and malt vinegar with a few other herbs thrown in and an incantation. The same incantation I just did on each of you. If a fairy comes at you, aim and squirt. According to the *Witchcraft – Spells and Potions* book, they hate the concoction. Everything seems to have worked thus far and I was reading this last night. I decided to make some just in case.'

'Where did you get the lemon balm?' asked Sandy.

'I gather it and store a large quantity. Mixed with mint, it makes for a good herbal tea,' replied Abigail, awkwardly looking her New Age geeky best.

'This is turning into a very uncanny afternoon indeed,' added Sandy, resigned to the next ordeal.

CHAPTER 18

SAY NIGHT, NIGHT TO THE FAIRIES

When the time finally came, Raymond saw his chance and took it without a moment's hesitation. The nurse with the medicine trolly had come out of Simon's single ward and was moving along the corridor towards the doorway of his ward, where there were six patients including himself. He quickly stepped out into the corridor and dodged the nurse's trolly coming towards him with its medicinal contents. He noticed Simon's cup and plastic mould that had contained his pills were both empty.

'Where are you off to, Mr Cheeseman? I have your medicine here,' said the young nurse.

'I'll be no more than two ticks, nurse,' Raymond replied, and then whispered, 'Just got to see a man about a dog.'

'Oh, I see,' replied the kindly young nurse. 'Well be as quick as possible, please. Your medication is here.'

'Will do, nurse,' he said and watched as she went into the ward.

He looked back at the reception desk and was pleased to see the ward sister wasn't there. He still wondered if there were matrons like in the *Carry On* comedy films. Or perhaps hospitals didn't have these old rankings anymore. Once again Raymond reminded himself, he couldn't keep up with the continuous changes in protocol. With determination and a swift, deceitful look around, he quickly opened the door to Simon's solitary ward and slipped in.

'What the blazes are you doing here?' came a whispered reply from Simon. He was on his side and had pulled himself up from his pillow.

Raymond was shocked that Simon Careful was conscious, but it was also apparent the man was still a little sedated.

'How are you feeling? I'm here for the same reason,' said Raymond.

Simon's eyes widened and then closed suspiciously. 'I doubt you have seen what I've encountered, mate. Even I don't believe what happened.'

Simon held a shaking hand before himself and looked at his tremoring fingers in disbelief, as though he might break down and start weeping at any moment.

'I know what you're going through,' whispered Raymond as he crept forward to Simon's bedside. Then he held up his bandaged wrist and continued, 'Those little creature things did the same thing to me as they did to you. There is a cure.'

Simon stared back at Raymond. It was an incredulous look of shock. 'Do you mean that you've seen the little things too? Those gorgeous little hideous things. Nasty little sods that giggle and chant. I do worry about them though. Why is that? I can't understand why. But I wish they'd come back,' he whispered sadly.

'I did see one of them, mate. Got kissed by the little thing too. That's it, you see. You can't let the things kiss you. It is a forever-smitten kiss. You'll be forever upset by this fake, lamenting torment when the impish thing runs off. I'd never experienced anything like it.'

'I know, it's incredible to feel this way. But how can anyone believe such a thing if they've never experienced it? How can they ever understand how much I care for them? Why am I so concerned for them? Why?' Simon was becoming repetitive. He might have been more anxious if it weren't for his past medication, the dose he had prior to the lemon balm concoction that the nurse had unknowingly given to him. Erstwhile medication with effects that were rapidly wearing off.

Raymond got out his crumpled piece of paper and asked, 'You did drink that horrible medicine, that the nurse just brought in, didn't you?'

'Yes, I did,' replied Simon as his face screwed up at the mere thought. 'It was bloody horrible.'

'Well, we're halfway there then. You'll be cured in a jiffy.' He grinned at Simon as he held the paper before him and awkwardly recited the Gaelic verse.

'*Bí imithe mites Domhan. Fill ar ais ar do fhearann.*'

'Pardon?' replied Simon, feeling a little confused.

'I'm told the results are rather quick and speaking from my own experience yesterday, the cure of all the melancholy feelings is very swift indeed.'

Simon sat upright and said, 'I can feel it. Even though I'm subdued with the drip medication.' He looked at the drip feed going into his arm. 'I can feel the emotional abandonment leaving me. Why on earth was I so hurt and distraught about some diabolical little hideous thing like that?'

'I know,' agreed Raymond. 'I felt a complete twonk when the wave of the potion and spell washed through me too.'

'That was bloody marvellous,' agreed Simon.

'Works a treat, don't it? My old girl's gone off to your place to make your wife and Sandy, that fruit-cake analyser woman, take the potion and hear the spell. Evidently the risk of little fairy folk dishing out kisses is still real. Also, there's a renewal of the spell on your house to keep the Little Wood folk at bay. I would have laughed about all of this a couple of days ago, but it seems that old man, Mr Ballantyne, was right.'

'Well, we can't stay here…' Simon lingered and realised he didn't know the man's name.

'Raymond Cheeseman, but you can just call me Ray,' answered Raymond in anticipation of Simon's difficulty.

'Oh right, Ray,' Simon replied. He remembered Janice telling him that Ray and his partner were affectionately known as Chalk and Cheese by the local people. 'My name is…'

'…Simon Careful,' completed Raymond. 'I know all of this too.'

'We've got to get back to the house and help the women, Ray. We have to get out of this place.'

'That wins my vote,' agreed Raymond. 'It's no good trying to discharge ourselves. We'll have all the furore of the nurses and doctors trying to dissuade us. We, in turn, can't argue our cause of wicked little fairies with infectious kisses. We're likely to bomb out on the persuasion stakes.'

Simon looked up from his hospital bed and sighed. 'No, that one is not going to work. Especially on that big ward sister sitting at the reception desk. Have you seen her?'

Raymond nodded in agreement. 'I know what you mean, mate. Her ponytail's got bigger biceps than any part of me.'

'Agreed,' said Simon. 'Bigger than your average Joe anywhere.' He thought the cheese aspect of the chalk and cheese couple was not such a bad fellow after all. In fact, he and Mr Cheeseman were both of the same mind and were speaking the same language. Ray was a sound fellow after all.

'So, you're game for a plan of action then?' Raymond had a big beaming smile on his face.

'We're singing from the same hymn sheet, Ray. I suggest we simply up and walk out of the ward. There's not a thing they can do to stop us.'

'Agreed, it's not as though they can physically restrain us.'

'Then it's to the rescue of our fair ladies,' said Simon enthusiastically, while looking down at the drip feed in his arm. 'I'll have to pull this thing out somehow.'

'Plus, the rescue of the well-intentioned fruit-cake analyser, your wife's friend,' added Raymond.

'Oh, Sandy. Is Sandy with them then?'

'Yes, she's the lady who struck up the friendship with my other half, Abigail. Wants me as a patient, complete with a course of colourful naughty smarties, no doubt.' Raymond walked around the side of Simon's bed to study the drip feed too.

At that precise moment, the ward door opened and the imposing six-foot-four-inch ward sister walked in with two younger nurses. The hospital sheriff and her trusted deputies.

'What is all this, Mr Cheeseman? I'm a little surprised at you.'

Simon, who was still partly light-headed from previous medication, didn't have much scope for a heated argument. He could talk a stern approach, but he was still rather lacking in his usual masculine resolve as of the moment. Also, the ward sister was even taller than first anticipated and a little broader when up close.

Raymond, on the other hand, had a rush of ill-deserved confidence. He often liked to flatter himself that he could talk his way out of most situations. And thus, he decided to try and induce such a circumstance at this particular moment, especially with an audience of subordinate deputy nurses. He might treat the young ladies to a display of how to deal with an overconfident ward sister who had the conviction of her own vanity. Give the old girl a bit of the old flannel, as he liked to put it. Let the young nurses sit back and enjoy the show. After all, it often worked on his kindly, easy-going partner Abigail. She was a rather laid-back lady. Perhaps this lent him an ill-deserved belief in his perceived lady-confrontational abilities.

Raymond puffed out his chest and began, 'I'm afraid, Simon and I are walking out of here, love. Sorry to be a pain but our minds are made up. No time for discharge forms and if there're no clothes, then it's with pyjamas and dressing gowns we go. Again, I'm sorry, love, but that's the way the pickle squirts on this one.'

One of the nurses went around to examine Simon's drip feed as Raymond smiled at the formidable ward sister looking down at him with eyebrows humorously raised. She had the look of a blond-haired version of the character actress Hattie Jacques from the *Carry On* comedy movies.

'I'm sure you are a fine "take charge lady" with the nurses. Fair enough – every respect for the important job you do. But my friend and I are out of here,' Raymond said with a cocksure attitude. He liked to flatter himself that he was a man of conviction. With Simon, he would have the task complete in the wink of an eye. No one was going to stop them.

'And just how do you get to wherever it is you are going in this snowy weather with no transport and no money for a taxi, Mr Cheeseman?' asked the ward sister, looking down with a contemptible grin at the skinny and unimpressionable man before her. She had dealt with many a cheeky old sod in her time and the one before her was small fry.

Raymond realised he hadn't thought of the weather and transport but he did have Simon Careful on board with the idea. Simon was certainly a man of means. He had a nice cottage in the woods and a rather nice-looking Audi SUV car of sorts. Simon could easily promise the taxi driver payment upon arrival of any said location.

'I'm sure Mr Careful and myself can work that little conundrum out for ourselves, lady.' He turned to Simon for support.

Raymond was a little shocked to see his recently acquired friend was fast asleep on his side with a contented smile on his face.

On the other side of the bed, behind the sleeping Simon, was the young nurse who had checked his drip feed. Now, she was awkwardly holding her empty syringe while pulling up the blissfully sleeping man's pyjama bottoms. Covering his recently exposed bottom. A posterior that had received the contents of the nurse's hypodermic.

'Oh!' said Raymond with a note of surprise. 'You've put him out.'

'Well, I'm certain Mr Careful will jump to the task once he's slept on the issue for a while, Mr Cheeseman,' replied the ward sister, while gently but firmly taking Raymond by the arm and leading him unceremoniously out of the solitary ward on his toes.

'Look, lady, Mr Careful and I have both had an ordeal but we're alright now. We are cured and will not do this silly stuff again.' He held up his bandaged wrist to her.

'Oh, that is so reassuring, Mr Cheeseman. No more upsets for you or Mr Careful. That is very encouraging news. Very encouraging, indeed. Do you not think so too, Nurse Philips and Nurse Rowe?'

'Oh, indeed we do,' said Nurse Philips, laughing while the other nurse just chuckled and smiled.

The formidable ward sister and the two nurses frogmarched the protesting man along the corridor to his ward.

'That's right, lady. My wife had a potion and a spell. They actually work, believe it or not. I wouldn't have believed it, but I do now. That's because I've witnessed it.'

'Oh,' patronised the awfully tall ward sister, 'that is good news. May I ask how your wonderful wife came about this potion and spell? And what did you actually witness?'

'She got the spell and potion that cures people from her book called *Witchcraft – Spells and Potions.*'

'Really?' she replied with a big condescending smile and a look to her two subordinate nurses. A look that said, 'We've got a live one, here.'

'And the things I've witnessed will make anyone's mind boggle,' added Raymond, seeming a little more desperate about his powers of sweet-talking women.

'You're preaching to the converted, Mr Cheeseman. 'I'm sure our minds are already boggling with anticipation.'

'I've been kissed by a fairy the same way as Mr Careful was, and that's what drove us crazy. The sense of loss when the little things skitter off into the woods and leave you will make any person resort to this type of desperation.' He once again held up the bandage around his cut wrist.

'Well, you certainly seem to be resorting to desperation,' added the ward sister.

He was led to his hospital bed by his entourage of caring ladies. All smiles and supporting compliance. The next thing Raymond knew, he was being laid down like a compliant puppy, the daunting ward sister looking down at him with Nurse Rowe standing beside her. Nurse Philips had gone around the bed as Raymond made one last effort to win over the resolute ward sister.

'Look, love, I know you may think I've pulled the odd stroke, but I'm not messing about. There are real, live fairies in the Little Wood a little way out of Lymington.'

He heard a few of the other patients chuckling behind him, while Nurse Philips had stealthily lowered his pyjama bottoms with well-practised ease.

Before the experienced Nurse Philips was a set of mottled and slightly hairy buttocks. Then with proficient ease, the nurse selected her target area. Casually, she injected the hypodermic's contents into one of the ample cheeks on offer.

'Ooh!' yelped Raymond as he stiffened.

The ward sister was smiling down at him as she said, 'Say night, night to the fairies, Mr Cheeseman.'

CHAPTER 19

THE ASSAULT ON THE CAREFUL'S COTTAGE

The three ladies and the black Labrador, Nelly, came out of the Side Wood and onto the icy pathway that led towards the front door of the Careful's cottage. Each woman was clearly shaken by the supernatural experience witnessed. All were in the process of coming down from the disturbing events as they emerged, once again, into the intense snowfall. The blizzard was as prevalent as ever. Yet it had a settling feeling as the cold snowflakes landed upon each lady's face. The women made their way up the slippery path, the front door making for a welcome sight.

'That seems a little cynical,' called Janice through the snow as she pointed to the sign over the letter box.

Abigail sniggered indulgently and agreed. 'Home Sweet Home is perhaps a little ironic. But it's also very welcome.'

'I wonder if your man has given my Simon that potion of yours?' added Janice as she pulled the street door key from her pocket.

'I wouldn't hold out too much hope of our gallant knights in shining armour making a bold appearance anytime soon,' said Abigail.

'Do you think your fella could get by all the scrutiny of the medical staff?' Janice was beginning to worry and a new look of doubt came over her face.

'I think Raymond might manage that, but I never gave him instructions about what to do next. Raymond always needs instructions. I think he'll get the spell and potion bit right but what to do after that wouldn't be in his remit, and I never told him to do anything beyond the potion and spell,' replied Abigail as she followed Janice up to the street door.

'Don't worry, I'm sure Simon will think of something. He likes to take a bull by the horns,' added Sandy, following them.

'I do hope you're right, Sandy,' added Janice.

'In the meantime, let's prepare for the little rascals. I'm certain they'll try to get into the house. My spell for this is a bit long-winded and I could be interrupted. I must concoct a second clearance spell with the dead raven and the brick again,' added

Abigail as she pulled out her old book from her heavily laden bag.

The door opened and Janice stood back allowing Abigail and Sandy to enter first. She looked out towards the Side Wood and noticed the rapid growth of green leaves close to the road where Abigail's Toyota Townace and Sandy's white Range Rover were parked.

'Look!' She pointed.

'That will be them,' said Abigail, looking at the green spread along the perimeter of the woods.

'Close the door, Janice,' added Sandy as she gently pulled her friend in. She closed the door and locked it.

'The landline! Try the landline phone,' said Abigail, checking her mobile again. There was no signal.

Janice and Sandy then removed their coats and hung them on the coat rack.

'I'll check it out now,' said Janice, going into the front room and picking up the phone receiver. 'The line's dead.'

'How do they do that?' asked Sandy as she looked through the letter box up at the telephone cable going to the outdoor pole. 'The line seems intact.'

'Please take your liquid-squirting bottles,' instructed Abigail. 'We're going to need all hands to the pump.'

Both Sandy and Janice pulled their plastic bottles from the coat pockets and looked to Abigail for approval.

'Just think of them as firearms that repel fairies. Very useful according to the instructions of the book.'

'Let's hope we don't have to use them,' said Sandy.

'I'll not hesitate,' added Janice. 'And I think they'll work. You've been right on these instructions from that strange book so far.'

Abigail smiled and nodded. 'I have another three bottles in the bag plus a selection of other goodies for the little confrontation that awaits us.'

'Bring it on,' said Sandy.

'Yes, let the little gits try and get in here,' Janice spat, getting angry at the thought of the little wraiths trying to invade her home.

Nelly whined, wanting to be in on the action too. Janice bent down and stroked the dog. 'You too, you wonderful mutt. You're a very valuable member of the group, Nelly.'

'Do any of the rooms have locks?' asked Abigail.

'All of the bedrooms do, the upstairs bathroom and so does the door to the cellar,' answered Janice.

'That's most helpful. Can we lock them immediately, please?' Abigail asked as she opened her book.

'I'll do the upstairs bedrooms,' said Sandy as she began to ascend the stairs.

Janice called up, 'You'll have to take the keys out from the inside of each room. Including the bathroom. They'll all be locked from outside on the landing instead of inside.'

'I've got that,' replied Sandy, confident of the task at hand.

Janice looked to Abigail. 'Mr Ballantyne kept all things the old way and Simon and I have had no chance to modernise.'

'Oh, there's no use telling me about modern things, Janice. I hope I may call you Janice…?'

'Of course, Abigail.' She laughed nervously.

'Raymond and I are not exactly your modern-day couple. As I'm sure you and Sandy may have guessed. We're total geeks and love being geeks. Although an assault by an army of fairies is perhaps a little geekier than I could ever have expected or wanted to indulge.'

Again, Janice laughed nervously. She was rather fond of Abigail's manner.

Further conversation was cut short by the din of far-off giggling coupled with the usual, all-too-familiar, uncanny infantile chanting.

'*La, la, la. La, la, la.*'

'Here they come again,' Sandy's voice called from upstairs. She could be heard systematically removing the bedroom keys from inside each room and locking each door from outside on the landing.

'*La, la, la. La, la, la.*'

'May I go into the kitchen?' asked Abigail, standing there with her book, brick and dead raven dangling on twine by its talons, her long-handled canvas shopping bag over her shoulder full of other things necessary for spell making.

'Of course, Abigail. This way, please.'

They made their way into the kitchen and could hear Sandy returning down the stairs. There was a table in the middle of the spacious area and Abigail put her dead raven upon it along with the book, the brick and her full shopping bag.

'I'm sorry about your nice clean table, Janice. However, the circumstances are dire at the moment.'

'Oh, that's fine,' Janice replied with a nervous giggle. 'I've got all the necessary cleaning things below the sink for later. It's the little sods outside I'm worried about. You know, I'm looking at all your strange things for making spells and only a day ago, I would have thought you a total fruit loop. But now I'm a total convert. Do whatever you need to do. We're relying on you totally, Abigail.'

'I've just locked the cellar door too,' said Sandy as she entered the kitchen and looked out of the window into the rear garden. Her mouth opened in shocked wonder.

'What is it?' asked Janice.

'Look!' She pointed into the garden.

'Oh, my word!' Abigail gasped.

Sandy exclaimed in panic, 'All the flower beds are in full bloom. The roses, the cornflowers, red hot pokers, even daffodils. So many different flowers.

'Spring and summer flowers all growing together in the conditions of a winter snowstorm!' Sandy was in a state of further bewilderment.

'*La, la, la. La, la, la.*'

'The little blighters must be all around the garden,' said Abigail, while returning to her book of spells and potions.

'I have done this particular spell on this place before for Mr Ballantyne, though not under these conditions. It was all rather relaxed before. I thought I was indulging the old man, but he insisted, in his own words, "It brought about an understanding of the strange little folk of the Little Wood."'

'Was it summertime?' asked Sandy.

'No, it was almost spring,' replied Abigail. 'But it had been snowing a few days earlier. Mr Ballantyne was insistent that the little rascals were more troublesome when it snowed. They couldn't kiss him and glimmer him anymore because of the counter spell I put upon him and upon the both of you. But these strange little folk still tried to torment him, like they're doing to us now. I thought I was just indulging him at the time with my spell book. I was thinking it would psychologically settle his mind.'

'So, these little things tried to gain access to Mr Ballantyne's home?' asked Janice.

'He said he managed to keep them at bay. He had two dogs at the time and locked himself in this kitchen. They got into the house according to him but left when the weather changed. Raymond and I didn't believe him. We just humoured him with these spells and thought it settled him. He suspected they came in via the cellar at night. His dogs kept waking him up and eventually he sought me out again, to do the home spell against fairy intrusion. Again, Raymond and I thought we were helping him from a psychological point of view. I believed he was disturbed. The spell a placebo effect that he convinced himself to believe.'

'But now we all know different,' said Sandy.

Abigail nodded her agreement. 'They'll try to access your home as and when they want. Especially at night when you want to sleep. It can be very intrusive as I'm sure you can imagine. This spell works for the owner of the home. Today it's you, Janice. It will stop them, but they mustn't be allowed to enter the nucleus area. I think that's this downstairs area somewhere. Mr Ballantyne said they got in here and began to cause the sleepless nights for him and his barking dogs.'

'Oh dear,' replied Janice. 'Nelly will go potty at the slightest sound.'

'We can stop them at all points of entry,' encouraged Sandy, patting the plastic squirting bottle. 'While Abigail buys us time with a displacement spell and then concocts the longer house-protection spell. Is that the plan of action?'

'Indeed, it is, Sandy.' Abigail smiled enthusiastically.

Outside, the chanting was getting louder and nearer.

'*La, la, la. La, la, la.*'

Abigail began to open the wings of the dead raven ready to add herbs and balm. 'This is their last opportunity. In snow they're more active and now they've kissed the owners of the cottage, they'll still try to claim the centre ground of your home. They're still emboldened.'

'It hasn't snowed like this for about five or six years,' said Sandy. 'Was that when Mr Ballantyne asked you to help him?'

'It was, actually. There's probably something in the snowstorm that encourages the little fiends to come out. Mr Ballantyne said he rarely saw signs of them in summer, but then things bloom naturally. There're no giveaway signs. Yet he often felt they were watching him.'

'Their chanting is getting louder,' said Sandy.

'*La, la, la. La, la, la.*'

'They're getting closer,' agreed Janice fearfully.

Nelly suddenly started barking at the locked cellar door. Her teeth bared in pure rage.

'They're in the cellar,' added Janice. 'They've been there before.'

Hideous little giggles came from the other side of the door. The little wraith-like beings were no doubt on the cellar staircase having gained entry via the cellar's upper fanlight window.

'Move about and keep a check on all the doors and windows,' instructed Abigail as she began to take out sealed jars with potions in and a small herb-crushing bowl with a herb grinder.

'Will you remain here with your things?' asked Sandy.

Outside, came the continuous giggling of high-pitched and excited voices coupled with the persistent chanting. Little hands patted the cellar door while Nelly kept up her barking.

'*La, la, la. La, la, la.*'

'Yes,' Abigail answered. 'I have the second fairy-displacement spell to do. It'll take a minute or two and that will buy us time for the protective house spell to be done. The displacement spell is the same one I did back in the wood when the little things tried to surround you. I need to sprinkle fresh herbal ingredients on the dead raven and repeat the incantation.'

'*La, la, la. La, la, la.*'

'Alright then, let's get to it,' said Sandy as she went out into the hall past Nelly. The front door's letter box was pushed in and up. Wicked pale-blue eyes peered in. Those of a supernatural being with minute, pin-sized black pupils.

Sandy moved a few steps forward. Behind her Nelly was barking at the giggling behind the cellar door and the chanting was growing stronger.

'*La, la, la. La, la, la.*'

A strong and determined sense of purpose gripped Sandy as she pushed the various noises from her cluttered mind. She focused on the wicked imp-ish eyes peering through the letter box and heard the nasty hissing from the mystical thing on the other side of the slot. She raised her plastic bottle quickly as she took aim. The squirt of lemon balm mixed with malt vinegar made her nostrils flare when the smell hit her. But the disgusted and angry retreating squeal from the outraged little creature on the other side of the letter box brought a sense of gratifying joy.

'Stick that in your pipe and smoke it, you little sod,' she called back as the letter-box flap slammed shut.

Janice had gone into the living room just in time to see a devious little fairy girl easing herself through the fanlight window of the living room.

The slight, impish thing wickedly looked down at her, a wave of ginger curls cascading down with delicate, pointed little ears protruding from each side of the tangled locks.

With controlled resolve, Janice held her squirting bottle up and let the little wraith-fairy get it full in the face.

'Chew on that, carrot top,' scolded Janice.

The horrid little thing screamed and retreated back through the fanlight, falling past the bay window outside onto the snow. The sprightly little bundle of cobwebbed-clothed mischief got up shaking her head. Then she ran out over the snow into the flower bed that bloomed in spectacular floral colour. Vibrant shades that excelled through the heavy snowfall.

'*La, la, la. La, la, la.*'

'They're upstairs in the bedrooms,' yelled Sandy.

Abigail called back, 'If the doors are locked leave them to it. Defend downstairs.'

As Abigail looked into her opened book, she once again read out a displacement spell over the dead raven.

'*Thosaigh wraith beag. Bí imithe ón gciorcal an toirt seo.*'

The raven was prepared and all she had to do was throw it outside and another protective fairy-free circle of about seventy yards radius would form temporarily. This would give them time for the house-protecting spell to be prepared before the angry mites regrouped and returned for another assault. Inside was no good. The dead raven had to drop on open land.

At that moment, the kitchen fanlight clattered and opened inwards. A slight-framed fairy boy with raven hair easily slipped in with acrobatic grace. The impish creature landed hands first on the kitchen worktop and turned head over heels, and out, to land faultlessly in an elegant and upright stance. There stood three and a half foot of slight, elfin-looking lad on the other side of the table from where Abigail worked.

Abigail smiled. 'Oh, I'm afraid an unwelcome brat like you will need to do a little better than that.'

The creature's little white ceramic face suddenly lost his wicked smile. It seemed confused by the woman's unimpressed reaction. She was not enchanted by his stare. His little mouth opened to reveal tiny fangs and a slithering forked tongue. It was clearly confused.

His slight, semi-naked form hesitated. It was a mere moment, but Abigail noticed it. Then the little creature slowly crouched as though making ready to leap, determined to deliver some expected mischief. The urchin was the complete scallywag in Abigail's unimpressed estimation.

'Oh, you are a little bounder, aren't you?' teased Abigail. 'Just look at you in your fine little cob-webbed loincloth. You're up against the big girls now, little one.'

Her squeezy bottle came up and shot a burst of lemon balm and malt vinegar into the fairy's face. The wraith squealed in anger and raised its tiny hands to his face. He had also alerted Nelly to his unwelcome presence. She had been barking at the locked cellar door knowing the little creatures were on the other side of it. Now the angry dog had one impish creature on full visual. There it was, standing in the kitchen – in Nelly's home – on her territory. She sprang at the little scoundrel with bared teeth, biting the troublemaker's arm. The screaming rascal jumped up on the kitchen top and quickly hauled himself back up to the fanlight. Nelly took another opportunistic leap, her teeth sinking into one of the fairy's depart-ing fleshy little buttocks. Another squeal of pain as the impish lad exited the fanlight and fell past the window outside.

Abigail heard the thud, and the muffled yelp. Then she watched the wounded urchin scamper off into the vibrant winter flowers.

'Dashed well done, Nelly. Good girl,' added Abigail as she picked up her dead raven. 'Here we go for the next part of this little battle.'

Sandy was still in the hallway, squirting a raven-haired fairy girl who was attempting to enter via a fanlight window next to the street door. She had waited for the little wraith to get her form halfway in. Then Sandy, with a gratified smile, squirted the impish thing full blast in the face. The much-hated anti-fairy substance of lemon balm, vinegar and a concoction of unknown herbs hit the spot.

The naughty little thing screamed in abhorrent disgust and shot backwards the way she'd come.

'Another one bites the dust,' she called as Abigail stood beside her with the dead raven and brick.

'This is what blokes might call, heavy artillery,' said Abigail.

Janice came into the hallway from the living room. 'I've taken out two. They seem to like the fanlights.'

Abigail nodded approvingly and said, 'We're about to throw this fairy-dispersal spell into the front garden. It'll create a temporary fairy-free zone of about seventy yards radius. It'll incorporate the entire house and beyond. Then we must use the time to get the house spell sorted.'

'Before the little sods come back?' asked Sandy.

'Indeed,' replied Abigail. 'Get ready to open the door and stand by with squirt bottles.'

'Ready?' asked Sandy with one hand poised on the door latch and the other holding her squirt bottle ready.

Abigail and Janice stood with their squirt bottles poised. Abigail's other hand firmly clutched the brick and dead raven against her rainbow cardigan.

'Ready,' they both agreed.

Sandy pulled the door open as each woman went to spray any would-be fairy at the doorstep. There was nothing. Just the intense snowfall outside and the chanting.

'*La, la, la. La, la, la.*'

'The flowers are still growing through the snowfall. They're out there somewhere,' said Janice.

'The little sods are definitely out there somewhere,' added Sandy.

A sudden hissing from many directions. The appearance of screaming fairies attacking their immediate position. A charge that caused each lady to start. A boy fairy swung in from above like a gymnast as two more fairies hiding either side of the doorway shot into the hallway.

Abigail managed to squeeze off a squirt of the hated balm solution. Then she was clattered by the swift swinging form of the little fairy boy with white hair. The slight frame bounced off of Abigail's larger and stronger figure. The roguish little lad fell back holding his hands to his eyes and in apparent discomfort. Abigail's balm had found its mark. Beyond came the relentless infantile chanting as the battle of the front door commenced.

'*La, la, la. La, la, la.*'

Janice squirted her squeezy bottle at a fair-haired female wraith. The impish thing coming in from her side of the door. She followed up the liquid splash and clouted the little pixie minx with a hard slap on top of the head. The angry little thing squealed and hit the floor before quickly crawling backwards hissing and spitting outside into the snow.

Sandy was holding up a scallywag boy fairy who was dangling, kicking and thrashing, by his ginger locks. She was shaking him angrily and squirting her lemon balm full in the urchin's face at point-blank range. The little blighter was squealing to be released as Sandy turned it back to the open door and unceremoniously kicked the thing up the backside and out into the blizzard.

'*La, la, la. La, la, la.*'

Before the fallen white-haired fairy despatched by Abigail had a chance to gather his wits, he was grabbed around the neck by Janice who then used her other hand to take a firm grip of his cobwebbed loin-cloth. She lifted the squealing little scallywag by neck and seat of his ragged cloth and walked the kicking and dangling lightweight rascal to the open doorway.

'Awe,' winced Abigail, 'that's one heck of a wedgy, Janice.'

Sandy and Abigail watched as the lady of the house launched the little imposter into the blizzard.

The urchin cartwheeled across the snow and stood up spitting and hissing back at his lady assailant. Yet the little scoundrel lacked the courage to return against such formidable opposition. She stood back, swiping her hands up and down.

'*La, la, la. La, la, la.*'

'That's sorted that little drama out,' she spat, though her voice trembled. She was trying to put on a brave face.

'Stand aside, girls,' said Abigail as she stepped forward to the open door and slung the brick and tethered raven with an under-arm cast, almost like a veteran soldier slinging an extra heavy hand grenade.

All watched in awe as the raven and the brick twisted out into the snowstorm. Arching out and quickly losing trajectory. It landed with a thump on the snow-covered lawn of the front garden. There followed a magical atmospheric ripple from the area where the dead raven's carcass landed. A distorted wave of air fanned out, made more visible as the falling snowflakes were violently displaced by the expanding roll of force. The boy fairy that Janice cast out was knocked down again, the brief energy surge covering every approach to the cottage.

'Like a ripple on a still morning lake,' muttered Abigail, satisfied.

They watched as the ghastly fairy boy stood and ran for the Side Wood to be away from the spell's nasty surge.

'That bag of slugs and snails is off with his puppy dogs' tails,' Abigail said, laughing.

The surge stopped the chanting abruptly but there followed squeals of hidden, angry high-pitched voices. Unearthly hisses and groans of the strange creatures protesting amid the uncanny winter-blooming flowers.

'Dins of eerie disapproval,' yelled Abigail frumpishly.

'Well, it's nice to see you enjoying yourself, Abigail,' replied Sandy nervously.

They watched and listened to the abating discord. A retreat of protest and the sad sight of perishing flowers, decomposing in an instant. Everywhere, the sad, withering brown petals began to fall and become instantly covered by the continuing snowfall.

'Close the door please, Sandy,' advised Abigail as she stepped back. 'Now for the final task and the completion of the home-protecting spell, before the little blighters come back.'

'The late Mr Ballantyne certainly had a point,' Sandy gasped.

'None of you believed him?' Janice stated, bemused. 'I'm sure I wouldn't have either. But now…? While we were fighting the wicked little things, I was charged up with aggression. Now it is over, I'm shaking.'

'It's not over yet, Janice,' added Sandy, feeling just as anxious.

Janice shook her head in disbelief. She was sweating. Her face an expression of complete shock. She looked up at Sandy holding out her hands in supplication.

'Outside, it's still bitter cold and snowing. Inside, it's stuffy and claustrophobic – dreadfully so,' she said.

'We must see this through, ladies,' added Abigail. She was coming down from the adrenalin rush. 'We all find our circumstance difficult to trust, each of us wanting to find an excuse for the bizarre and supernatural experience. But there is none. It has happened! The wraith-like sprites have attacked the cottage. They almost breached the defences to find the sweet spot.'

Nelly whined as she looked up at them from by the cellar door where the faithful mutt stood committed to her guard duty.

'Nelly always goes back to the cellar door. She seems riveted to that spot,' said Sandy.

'She's protecting the cellar access,' answered Janice.

'It could also be the sweet spot,' replied Sandy. 'Perhaps Nelly has a better understanding of the situation than we give her credit for.'

Abigail was adjusting quickly. She spoke next, 'If the book is right, and I see no reason to dismiss it, these horrid little things will be back once the displacement spell runs down. We saw this in the Side Wood and it will reoccur around this cottage. They want the sweet spot of the property and the spell will take longer to concoct than most. It did last time. Let's leave Nelly to her own way. Let's accept she knows something. She certainly has the cellar door covered.'

Abigail turned and went back to the kitchen, where her preparation equipment and spell book were on the table.

'I'll stay by the front-room window,' added Sandy.

'I'll take the back door, and I can watch along the hall for the front door too,' added Janice.

Abigail called back from the kitchen where she made her preparations, 'I'll need about six to seven minutes. I think the displacement will last for about four minutes. Then there could be a rush. Just like last time, but perhaps more intense. Stand ready with the squeezy bottles.'

'Our cheap-shop washing-up liquid bottles? Ones that're not soft and gentle with real Fairy liquid repellent?' joked Sandy.

'Oh indeed, that's the ones.' Abigail laughed with her New Age nerdy girl enthusiasm bubbling to the fore.

Sandy and Janice anxiously maintained their watchful duty and were encouraged by the sound of Abigail moving various utensils.

The women needed to speak to one another. The tension was building to an unbearable point. Each knowing that soon the mischievous little fairies would return.

Sandy checked the fanlight windows, her hands firmly clasping her plastic washing-up liquid bottle. Her much coveted anti-fairy weapon. She called back, 'I must say, it is encouraging to hear that clinkering and stirring, Abigail. It lends confidence that we're getting prepared.'

'Yes, and the pouring of potent liquid,' said Janice, laughing nervously from the hallway by the back door. She also clasped her plastic spray bottle.

'It is rather gratifying to be of service, ladies,' Abigail replied nervously. 'I think the next attack will be a tad more desperate. They need to do something at the sweet spot of the house. It must be down here and I think Sandy might have a point about Nelly's position by the cellar door. The dog seems glued to the spot and the potential entrance via the cellar. Almost as though Nelly is preparing to make a last stand there.'

Again, Nelly made a low-pitched whine. The devoted black Labrador was sitting there in the hallway, knowing the ladies were talking about her.

The faithful mutt could see Abigail in the kitchen, Janice to her side and also Sandy through the living-room door.

'How do these little things claim this sweet spot of the house?' called Janice.

'I think they have some form of a standard or pendant,' replied Abigail.

'Does it mean I would lose my house?' asked Janice.

'No, but the little mites could access it as and when they wanted. I think the late Mr Ballantyne realised they were just being intrusive and extremely irritating. That's why he came back to me concerning the second spell, a few days after I had done the first.'

'The first being the one to stop the smitten kiss?' called Janice. 'The one you did to cure me?'

'That's correct,' answered Abigail.

The three ladies needed the small talk. It was important and built courage. It kept their stressful waiting situation nicely stoked for the ordeal that would surely come.

'So, if they put the pendant or standard thing in the sweet spot, what happens with my house?' Janice was getting nervous at the prospect.

'The spell I'm making would still work but I would prefer to stop them now. Rather than you and Simon having more sleepless nights. It caused

Mr Ballantyne no end of problems before the home spell was done, even though their smitten kisses could no longer work on him,' concluded Abigail.

'Are you still going to stay at the cottage then, Janice?' asked Sandy bemused from her position at the window of the living room.

'Of course,' replied Janice. 'I'm not being driven out. I don't think Simon will either. There was something in that fairy kiss. The silly yearning for their company is gone, but there's a steadfast will not to let the little buggers have their wicked way.'

Abigail chuckled. 'That is exactly what Mr Ballantyne said. I think he developed a rapport with them after a time. A mutual respect of sorts. Raymond and I thought we were just indulging a senile old man, but it seems the old boy was anything but. He loved his cottage all the more and developed this understanding with the strange folk of the Little Wood.'

'Maybe Simon and I will too?' muttered Janice hopefully. 'I don't want to leave this place. Despite what's happening.'

'Oh my God!' called Sandy from her position overlooking the front garden. 'There are sunflowers growing in the snow. Huge beautiful sunflowers. Cornflowers and hollyhocks too. The flora is creeping closer.'

The faint sound of chanting resumed and began to get louder.

'*La, la, la. La, la, la.*'

'Out the back too,' called Janice. 'Roses, lavender, wisteria, foxglove and hydrangea. My word it's very striking.'

'*La, la, la. La, la, la.*'

'A slight touch of the Percy Thrower's there, Janice. No time for that sort of thing. It's little fairies we're looking for. And they are out there behind those winter blooms and probably sneaking closer.'

'What are the Percy Thrower's?' Janice replied, wondering if it was something to do with Abigail's older age.

Nelly started to bark at the cellar door. Intruders had entered downstairs behind the locked door. Upstairs, the fastened bedroom doors started to rattle again, a new and desperate intensity, yet not with the strength of human beings.

In the living room, Sandy jumped back from the bay window as two girl fairies suddenly and nimbly jumped out of the foliage onto the outdoor windowsill. One with thick and wavy strawberry-blond hair, while the other had thick and wavy raven hair. Their impish blue eyes blazed against white ceramic-looking doll skin. Tiny, pin-sized black pupils looked at her from deep-blue irises. Each little minx had little pointed ears protruding from their hair and wet-looking dragonfly wings splaying out. The impish things started to push and probe at the fanlights.

Searching for any form of weakness. The sprites were dressed in the usual shredded cobweb frocks that had a delicate sheen. Tiny sparkles flared here and there amid the ragged garments. Each wraith was no more than three feet in height and both hissed with wicked, fanged grins. Inquisitive reptile-like stares and little forked tongues shot in and out.

'Come for the booby prize, you little scallywags,' muttered Sandy, holding up her squeezy bottle.

'*La, la, la. La, la, la.*'

There appeared to be a hesitancy of each little fairy. As though knowing Sandy held something disagreeable.

At the rear of the house, Janice jumped back when she heard a thump against the back door. Then at the upper square frosted windows, she made out a little ginger-haired head. One of the gremlin males.

'*La, la, la. La, la, la.*'

The cacophony of noise was growing in intensity and further championed by Nelly's barking.

Janice pushed the discord into the background and watched the short, matted clumps of ginger hair through the frosted-glass panels, vibrant locks sticking out like stalagmites in various directions, moving upwards past each square section. Towards the door's central square of glass, that was clear. A pane that was replaced with the wrong type of cut-glass from the past. A job to correct for the summer.

As the urchin's porcelain face passed over the plainer square glaze, Janice made out the pale-blue irises and the tiny, pin-hole pupils. The little urchin had a fixed grin that displayed spiteful little fangs with the usual forked tongue resting on his bottom incisor teeth.

The waif looked up at the fanlight and stretched its thin little arm while climbing the outer door. As the creature pushed, the fanlight gave way. The adventurous little ragamuffin shot up, needing no time to dwell on the matter. Within a split second the fairy's head was inside the opening and it peered down into the nozzle of Janice's squeezy bottle. A quick blast of the lemon balm concoction hit the fairy squarely in the face. The ill-intentioned intruder shot back as quickly as it came, screeching and hissing during the fall past the small back windows. There was a thump as the mite's body landed. Then more hissing as she heard the little creature scurry away.

Nelly's growling and barking became fiercer as she stood on her hind legs against the cellar door. The hidden intruders on the other side muttered unfathomable high-pitched murmurs, as though becoming cautious of what might await them.

In the kitchen, Abigail was working away busily. Not taking any notice of the three wraiths outside on the kitchen windowsill. Two boys and a girl all grinning and hissing, displaying their transparent dragonfly wings. A spectre of rainbow colour reflecting on the surface of the girl fairy's wing. Beyond, the snow continued to cascade amid the relentless chanting and Nelly's continued barking.

'*La, la, la. La, la, la.*'

'Look, look into my eyes,' the girl fairy said, mimicking the voice of the old man who had lived there. They were like parrots imitating noises they had heard before.

'Oh, we are a collection of impersonators, aren't we?' Abigail smiled back at the three scallywags outside as she continued with her concoction. Adding herbs and taking the simmering water with lemon balm and pouring it into her mix. Peering over to read further instructions from her book.

'Not long now, my little delinquents. Be patient and you might end up with likeable neighbours. You grew to like Mr Ballantyne, didn't you?'

One of the boy fairies got halfway through the fanlight and reached down for the side window's latch. He managed to pull it up just as Abigail shot a long-distance blast of lemon balm from her squeezy bottle. The lad's shrill outburst told of angry disapproval. The fairy shot back out and fell from the windowsill. Abigail lowered the squeezy bottle and continued with her concoction making. Unaware that the side window was now loose.

'Almost done,' she shouted as the side window was yanked open and the female fairy shot through followed by the remaining male wraith. The little woman landed beside Abigail while the rogue-looking male came down on the other side of the table.

Abigail reached for the squeezy bottle as the little lassie tried to grab her arm. The fairy was no stronger than an unruly brat of a child and lifted easily from the ground as Abigail held the squeezy bottle aloft. The brattish fairy still tried to stretch up and grab the plastic bottle from Abigail's raised hand. The little imp kicking and thrashing as she dangled, hissing through her forked tongue and splaying her delicate, transparent wings in an aggravated manner.

'We have a breach in the kitchen,' shouted Abigail.

Instantly, Janice appeared. A blast of lemon balm forced the girl fairy to drop and scurry away beneath the table. Abigail lowered her raised arm and aimed at the boy fairy. She squeezed off a short burst into the scallywag's face and there followed another disapproving hiss.

'Another.' Abigail pointed to the open kitchen window where Janice recognised the returning ginger-haired scamp attempting to enter the cottage for a second time.

'You, don't learn, young man,' she said and blasted the urchin again. As before, the fairy boy retreated. He jumped backwards out into the snowy swirl and was consumed by the white of the snowfall. No doubt looking for a safer entry point.

The kitchen was still not fairy free and Abigail lifted her mixing bowl just in time. The two fairies taking cover beneath stood up. They pushed the table over and the remaining contents spilled and toppled across the kitchen floor.

'I need to say the incantation over the potion and start to spill small drops here and there around the sweet spot while doing so. We need these beastly little things out.'

'Where did you do it last time? When Mr Ballantyne was alive?' asked Janice, desperately spraying at the cowering boy fairy.

'All along the hallway and where Nelly is on guard,' replied Abigail.

Nelly was still at her spot by the cellar door barking and growling for all she was worth. All around was the infantile chanting. Even coming up from the cellar and from the locked bedrooms upstairs.

'*La, la, la. La, la, la.*'

The dog had seen the two fairy imposters in the kitchen, but on this occasion, she would not dare to leave the cellar door – as though she knew something more important was beyond.

'Go to it then, Abigail,' shouted Janice as she grabbed the little fairy male by the hair and squirted another dose of lemon balm into the rogue's squinting face. He squirmed and jumped up onto the sink and scurried on all fours for the open window. Janice let the male fairy get away as she turned her attention to the female sprite. The little imp looked visibly scared now and jumped up to the sink of her own free will and shot out of the open window, following her male companion. Janice quickly closed and latched the window.

In the hallway, Abigail was doing her chanting while slinging water about like scattering seed.

'*Ar an gcéad dul síos. Ní féidir le haon sióga dul isteach.*

'*Don dara cás. Ní féidir le haon sióga dul isteach.*

'*Don tríú cás. Ní féidir le haon sióga dul isteach.*'

Abigail stopped by Nelly, who was still barking at the cellar door. The chanting was fading as she said the final words, '*Anois bain go deo.*'

And then it all stopped. Including Nelly's barking. No more chanting, no more rattling bedroom doors, no sound except for a low-key whine from Nelly.

'The flowers are withering again,' called Sandy excitedly from the living room.

'The same out back in the garden,' Janice confirmed optimistically.

Then followed the silence. A quiet that screamed at the three women. A normal forest-cottage quiet that seemed eerie after the event they had been through.

'I think this is going to take a while for us to adjust,' said Abigail.

Sandy called from the living room. 'The landline is working again. We can call out.'

Each lady delved into their various pockets and pulled out their mobile phones. All were online and working.

'We can't exactly call the police,' said Abigail.

'What an earth would we say to them?' said Sandy, laughing.

'I'm still pinching myself,' added Janice.

'What now?' asked Sandy.

'Perhaps a tidy up and then a visit to the hospital to see Raymond and Simon?' suggested Abigail.

'That one works for me,' said Janice as she began to remove various cleaning products from beneath the sink.

Sandy and Abigail helped the lady of the house. They put every displacement back in order and cleaned the kitchen floor and sides. They also went into the hallway and hoovered up. Room by room, everywhere was checked, everywhere in the house.

CHAPTER 20

THE SETTLED DECISION

'I know they are no longer here,' said Janice. 'I can feel their presence is gone.' She put her coffee cup down.

'You can't stay here all night on your own, Janice,' Sandy replied. She was still blowing her hot coffee.

Abigail sipped her tea. 'Not wise for tonight, Janice. Not after what you've been through.'

Janice sniggered politely. 'I'm very grateful to the both of you for what you've done to help me. But I'm not scared. I know I should be, but the thought of fairies no longer spooks me. I know they are real. While we were confronting them, I was very anxious about the house. But now Abigail has done this spell, I know the place is safe. I know fairies are just little pests. Little mischief-makers that shouldn't be tolerated in the house. Maybe there will be an understanding. But I have no fear of them now. Not anymore.'

Abigail smiled. 'I think Sandy is concerned for you being alone. I understand what you mean, but perhaps for a day or two. Would it not be comforting to have a friend by your side?'

'I wouldn't expect Sandy to want to…'

'I would feel better if you let me stay while Harry is in Ireland. He comes back Wednesday evening. Tonight, and tomorrow, Janice. Just to make sure all is well?'

Janice smiled at her friend. 'Well of course, Sandy. I just didn't want to put on you.'

All laughed the matter off, knowing that Sandy would remain for a couple of days. It would give time for the dust to settle. Once that small issue was sorted out, the women returned to the next concern. Abigail's and Janice's husbands in the nearby hospital.

'A rough plan needs to be worked out by all three us,' Sandy suggested.

'I want Nelly to come with us. I don't think she should be left alone. Not for the moment,' said Janice, expressing her concern.

'Nelly will have to come too. I can remain in Abigail's people carrier while you two visit your husbands,' added Sandy.

Abigail nodded her agreement. 'I'll be armed with a fairy-smitten repellent, just in case Raymond hasn't been successful approaching Simon in the hospital. Though I think Raymond may have pulled it off with the potion. He can be deliciously sneaky at times. But it is best to make sure. He isn't answering his phone – perhaps he's sleeping.'

'I wonder what they'll say about this ordeal?' added Sandy. 'Simon and Raymond were converts before we were.'

'I think their faces will be a picture.' Janice laughed. 'At least we know why they did their awful thing. We also know they can be cured.'

Abigail looked at Sandy. 'Perhaps their mental health councillor will have the ultimate understanding too?' she said, laughing.

Sandy lifted her eyebrows jovially. 'Oh, I certainly think the counselling body will have a sympathetic assessor.'

Outside, the snow continued to fall. The last efforts of a robust winter. Soon the spring would come and Janice knew she was going to enjoy her little cottage in the New Forest, her old school friend close by and her new Wiccan friend too. The Little Wood would remain with its mysteries so. Hopefully with its little folk resorting to their more elusive existence.

Printed in Great Britain
by Amazon